Harlow Brewster had purchased the North Basin grasslands from the Shoshoni fair and square—and paid for the land with blood. So the boss of the Lazy 8 wasn't about to see a bunch of nesters turn his range into a plowed-up dustbowl. If the law couldn't get rid of the grangers, Brewster would make his own law. With a couple of loads of buckshot and a stout piece of hanging rope . . .

LYNCHER'S MOON

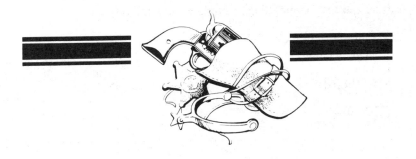

Will C. Knott

ATLANTIC LARGE PRINT
Chivers Press, Bath, England.
Curley Publishing, Inc.,
South Yarmouth, Mass., USA.

Library of Congress Cataloging-in-Publication Data

Knott, Bill, 1927–
  Lyncher's moon / Will C. Knott.
    p. cm.—(Atlantic large print)
  ISBN 0–7927–0167–4 (lg. print)
  1. Large type books. I. Title.
  [PS3561.N645L96 1990]
  813'.54—dc20
                                       89–29339
                                          CIP

British Library Cataloguing in Publication Data

Knott, Will C. (Will Cecil) *1927–*
  Lyncher's moon.
  I. Title
  823'.914 [F]

  ISBN 0–7451–9739–6
  ISBN 0–7451–9751–5 pbk

This Large Print edition is published by Chivers Press, England, and Curley Publishing, Inc, U.S.A. 1990

Published by arrangement with Berkley Publishing Group

U.K. Hardback ISBN 0 7451 9739 6
U.K. Softback ISBN 0 7451 9751 5
U.S.A. Softback ISBN 0 7927 0167 4

LYNCHER'S MOON

CHAPTER ONE

TEXAS, 1869

Harlow Brewster sat his horse ramrod straight. His dark eyes were smoldering as he looked down into the moonlit valley. The nester had completed his sod shack. Already its pestilential influence was visible on the valley's lush floor. It had taken an acre of sod, at least, to construct the soddie. Brewster could see clearly in the moonlight the patch of soil laid open to the sky after the nester's grass-hopper plow had finished slicing off the sod. The gleaming fragment of earth reminded Brewster of a brutal tear in a once-beautiful fabric.

Brewster was wearing a light, high-crowned Stetson. In the bright moonlight, his eyes gleamed from out of deep, shadowed sockets with only his thrusting jaw and thick, drooping mustache clearly visible. Eight riders—on horses as tall and deep chested as Brewster's—waited for Brewster to speak. Their high-strung horses stamped and shook their heads, their bits jingling. Otherwise there was no sound except the occasional squeak of good saddle leather as the men shifted their positions.

Brewster turned his head to address his

1

foreman. 'Fred,' he said, his powerful voice audible to every rider, 'you say the sonofabitch spent the entire day sodding that roof. He must have finished the sides last night then.'

The foreman, a lean, raw-boned man in his early twenties, nudged his horse closer to Brewster and nodded in agreement.

'The sides were up when I checked this morning. The four of them have been working on the roof all day, I figure. The two younger ones were hauling willow poles from the creek in the morning and must have spent the rest of the day digging up clay from the creek bank. The nester finished off the roof with a final dressing of sod, grass side up, over the clay. Mr. Brewster, this ain't the first soddie this nester ever built, I'm thinking.'

Brewster looked back down at the sodbuster's pitiful hovel. The first good rattling downpour would cause the roof to leak like an overloaded sponge. No matter how tight he had constructed the damned thing, field mice would tunnel through the walls, with garter snakes following close behind. Soon after would come the bed bugs and fleas.

But these nesters wouldn't mind.

They would stick it out and breed like rabbits. They didn't know any better. Only after they had plowed up his land and killed the grass waiting for the rain to show—only

2

when they had begun to starve while they watched the creek dry up, as it would in this flat, dry country every third or fourth year—only then would they join with others of their kind and start killing Brewster's beef to stay alive.

But Brewster did not intend to wait that long. He knew of other spreads that had waited. The nesters had flocked in, drawing more and more into the trap until their damned little homesteads covered the grasslands like warts on a toad's back. And Brewster had seen what remained of the land when the broke and starving nesters abandoned their shacks and sod dugouts and moved on like locusts to despoil other ranges—with their growing litters and their foolish, idiot reliance on the plow.

'God damn their eyes,' Brewster said softly, bitterly. 'I warned them.'

'That's right, Mr. Brewster,' Fred said nervously. 'You sure did.'

'You were with me. You heard what I told them. They were warned, good and proper.'

Fred nodded quickly, then glanced back at the other hands. Their faces were lean and hard in the moonlight. They had been priming all day for this night's action. They did not like sodbusters any more than Harlow Brewster did.

'Let's go,' said Brewster, nudging his powerful buckskin forward.

3

Before Brewster pulled up, the nester was out of the sod house, standing in front of the open doorway, a rifle cradled in his arms. Brewster was mildly surprised. When he had spoken to the nester earlier, he had seen no sign of firearms—and the fellow had not struck him as being a man very handy with weapons. As the nester watched him pull up now, Brewster saw the frightened way the man squared his shoulders. From the look of him, he was probably pissing in his pants.

Brewster pulled up within a few feet of the nester and leaned his high, square-shouldered frame forward over the pommel. 'You don't scare easy, is that it, Peterson?' Brewster said, chucking his hat back off his forehead and smiling coldly down at the nester.

'That's right, Brewster,' the man replied, his voice high, quavering. 'You can't turn me off like I was some stray dog! I bought this land and it's mine.'

'I know. You told me that before. But I told you what you can do with that deed, now didn't I?'

'You can't run me off,' the man repeated doggedly, his eyes moving unhappily from Brewster to the other hands now lined up alongside the cattleman.

'Yes, I can, Peterson. I have to. This land's

no good for farming. It's good for only one thing. Growing grass and running cattle. If you stay, you'll only starve. You know that better than I do.'

'What's that supposed to mean?'

'Why did you leave Oklahoma Territory?'

'We had three dry years in a row.'

"And you ended up eating your seed to stay alive. That about it?'

The granger took a step toward Brewster. 'And then came the locusts! The sky was filled with them. They ate the leather off the harnesses! It was a plague!'

'Well, Peterson, you're not going to ruin this grassland. You're not going to plow it up and leave it like them locusts. This is high, dry country. There is not enough rainfall for steady cropping here—any more than there was where you come from.'

'But ... but there's water here!' The man nodded eagerly toward the creek. 'Plenty of water!'

'This creek is dry as often as it is wet. Listen to me, granger. I know this country.'

'But the railroad said the rain follows the plow.'

Brewster's laugh was a short, mirthless bark of derision. 'And you believe everything the railroads tell you, do you.'

The man's thin face hardened. 'I ain't gonna believe what *you* tell me. And that's for sure.'

5

'I told you not to build here, Peterson,' Brewster said wearily. He was tired of trying to reason with this gullible fool. 'And now I just explained to you why you can't stay on my range.'

'This ain't your range!'

'My father took it from the Comanche,' Brewster said softly, 'and he paid for it with his blood. Spilling yours to keep it won't be pleasant. But if you force me, I won't have any choice.'

The granger's face paled. The softness of Brewster's tone coupled with the obvious weariness of the man alerted the granger to the fact of Brewster's short fuse. The nester looked from Brewster's face to those of his riders. Each man stared back implacably at him without the faintest hint of compassion or understanding. For a desperate foolish moment, Brewster realized, the man considered bringing his rifle up and firing on them. And then the moment passed. Brewster's estimation of the man had been correct. He had no real stomach for gunplay.

'You're moving out tonight, Peterson,' Brewster told him. 'You and your family. Go on back in and get your trunks filled up. And leave that rifle out here. Go on, now. You know I mean it.'

'Move out? *Tonight?*'

'I warned you not to build here.'

'But—'

'My men will help you load your wagons. We'll escort you to Dexter. We'll see you get there, all right. And that you keep on going.'

Peterson hesitated a moment. His backbone stiffened slightly, his shoulders inching back. Then he gave up. His shoulders sagging, he flung the rifle down, turned, and went back to the sod house.

Brewster leaned back in his saddle as he watched the man go, the tension easing out of him. He heard the creak of saddles about him as his men relaxed also. It was a hard thing Brewster was doing; but he was convinced absolutely that what he was doing for this granger, brutal and uncompromising as it was, would someday be looked back upon by the granger with gratitude. He had not lied to the man. This was no land for the plow.

The moment the granger disappeared into the doorway Brewster saw the flash of something metallic being thrust into his hands. Uttering a cry of warning, Brewster clawed for his six-gun as the granger whirled in the doorway. He was holding a double-barreled shotgun. One barrel belched flame. Brester felt the sting of buckshot as it whipped past his left cheek and heard the awful thunk as the load caught his forearm chest high. Some shot struck Fred's mount also. The animal whinnied in terror and reared suddenly, sending Fred tumbling backward off his horse.

7

By that time Brewster's gun was out and blazing, his head low over his horse's neck as he spurred the animal sharply to one side. The second barrel of the shotgun belched, and Brewster felt a sudden, heavy fist slam into his thigh. The force of the buckshot knocked his horse to one side. The animal stumbled and went down. Pulling himself free of the stirrups, Brewster rolled clear of the horse and came up firing at the doorway.

His riders too were pouring fire at the nester. His long frame caught against the rough doorjamb, the man was bucking loosely as each round slammed into him. Falling clumsily foward on what was now a heavy, strangely numb right leg, Brewster pumped one last round into the collapsing figure in the doorway.

Dimly he heard screams from inside the sod house. He tried to tell his men to quit firing, but his throat was uncommonly dry. He caught a glimpse of something white darting forward from the darkness of the house to grab the nester. He managed a strangled cry of warning to his men, but it came too late as the nester's woman was blown away by the withering fire. Then, from the window, came rifle fire. Brewster saw one of his riders buckle forward over his saddle horn. At once his men turned their fire on the window. Chunks of sod flew into the air. The rattle of rifle fire from the house halted.

Brewster waved frantically at his men to cease fire. At last they heeded him, and as the last shot sounded from the milling crowd of mounted men, an awesome silence fell over the little valley.

Brewster pulled himself to a sitting position and looked quickly at his foreman and the other rider who had been shot from his horse. Both men were lying very quietly on the grass as the rest of Brewster's riders flung themselves from their horses and rushed to inspect the fallen men.

As one rider bent over him, Brewster looked up at him. 'Never mind me. How's Fred?'

'He's dead, Mr. Brewster,' the man told him bitterly. 'He got nearly cut in half by that charge of buckshot.'

'Bill's dead too!' a rider over the other one cried.

The riders straightened and turned to look down at Brewster. The bright moonlight revealed clearly the shock registered on each face. This was not how it was supposed to have come out. They had ridden to this valley to scare a nester and his brood. The fellow was supposed to have left without argument with his tail between his legs. And now Brewster was wounded and two of their own were dead.

Tim Foster was standing over Brewster. The young puncher was a favorite of the

9

cattleman. Tim looked unhappily down at Brewster and cleared his throat. 'You better get someone to look after that wound, Mr. Brewster.'

Brewster nodded. 'Sure, Tim. But right now I want someone to see to the house. Is anyone left alive in there? Go find out, will you, Tim?'

Tim turned and ran cautiously, his head down, toward the sod house. Gun drawn, he ducked inside. A moment later, he emerged, stepping carefully over the two bodies slumped before the doorway. Head down, he walked toward them. No one queried him. They did not need to ask Tim what he had found.

As the fellow pulled up in front of Brewster, Brewster said softly, 'Both boys dead?'

Tim nodded.

Brewster took a deep breath. His head was spinning now from the pain swarming up his thigh. He felt light-headed and knew why. He was losing blood. 'Bury them,' he rasped hoarsely. 'Bury the lot of them over in that patch of ground they cleared. Leave no markers. Nothing!'

The men frowned down at Brewster, but not one questoned the order.

'And tomorrow, I want a work party to come back here and pull this soddie down, carefully. Replace the sod over the patch of ground they took it from. I don't want any trace of these nesters left. That clear?'

The grim circle of men moved restlessly. A few glanced uneasily at each other.

'Now, someone get me a horse and help me mount up. I'm ridin' back. I don't want my boy to see me hurt like this. I don't want him asking questions. And I don't want any of you men breathing a word of this to him—or anyone else.' Brewster looked over at an older rider. 'Sam, maybe you better ride back with me.'

'Maybe we better stop that bleedin' first,' Sam said, moving closer and peering down at Brewster's ragged thigh.

'Just get me up onto a horse, then bring me a length of rawhide. I'll stop the bleeding myself.'

Sam had been with the cattleman since he came to Texas eleven years before and knew enough not to argue with Brewster. The tall, lean fellow moved back through the ring of men to find one of the two riderless horses.

Brewster glared up at the rest of the riders. 'You heard what I just told you,' he said. 'Clear out that house and bury them bodies. Get to it!'

'What about Fred and Bill?' one of the men asked. 'We bury them too?'

Brewster did not have to think long on that one. Frowning in misery, the moonlit night tipping crazily about his head in a drunken

11

spin, he nodded. 'Yes,' he managed. 'Bury them too.'

There was a sullen, unhappy mutter at that. Brewster understood their reluctance. 'Goddamn it!' he exploded. 'We can't let this get out! Bury Fred and Bill! Bury them *all*!'

The men turned and plodded toward the dim sod house. Brewster closed his eyes. A moment later he felt Sam's hands pulling him upright. He roused himself and dragged his damaged thigh over the cantle, then took the rawhide from Sam's fumbling hands and wound it tightly about his raw thigh. The pain was enough to awaken him completely. As soon as Sam was mounted beside him, he urged his horse forward.

The important thing, he knew, the really important thing was not to let Carl see him ride in like this. His boy must never know about this night's awful business.

★　　　★　　　★

Carl Brewster, astride the paint his father had given him that spring for his twelfth birthday, watched with eyes wide in shock and dismay as his father's men walked slowly toward the sodbuster's shack. Carl's heart was still thudding wildly, his breath coming in shuddering gasps.

He had seen his father go down at the first

12

volley and then had seen the two Box B riders pitch from their saddles. He had watched in horror as the sodbuster and his wife were cut down. And he knew now the fate of the granger's two sons, as well. When Tim had returned from the soddie with his head down, Carl had immediately understood. They were all dead. The whole family.

Earlier that day Carl had ridden over to watch the nesters build their house and had soon found himself helping the two boys dig for clay along the creek bank. One of them, Tod, had been a tall, shy bean-pole of a kid with deep blue eyes. His brother Frank had been shorter and chunkier, with dark, tousled hair that hung down over his eyes. He had been forever brushing the hair back off his forehead as he worked. Before Carl had ridden back, the nester's wife had given him a thick slice of freshly baked bread, spread with a generous layer of apple butter, and had thanked Carl warmly for his help...

The sight of his father mounting up alerted him. Carl knew instinctively that his father must not know what he had seen. He pulled his paint around and spurred the pony across the prairie toward home. As he galloped through the moonlit night thinking of what he had just witnessed, he found himself crying unashamedly.

CHAPTER TWO

WYOMING, 1884

Sheriff Jed Sanford threw his cards down disgustedly and glanced up from the green felt table. He was just in time to see Clyde Sukeforth and his wild son, Will, haul up in the Cattleman's doorway, the saloon's batwings flipping shut behind them. There was no doubt in Jed's mind who Sukeforth was looking for—and why.

'Deal me out, gents,' Jed said quietly, as Sukeforth and his son headed grimly across the sawdust-covered floor toward him. 'Looks like I got me some business.'

The three other players followed Jed's glance as Sukeforth pulled up beside the table and glanced balefully down at the sheriff. 'We been lookin' for you, Sheriff.'

Sukeforth had the look of a man who had never known a full meal—and the smell of one who had never known a bar of soap. His lean, almost skeletal face was seamed with dirt, his fingernails were black, and his bib overalls looked as if they had only recently been dragged through a muck pile. His smell was compounded of worked earth, horse manure and urine, hay, and axle grease. His son, a few inches taller than his father, was

14

well into his twenties and had the same famished, skeletal look about him. The difference was in his eyes. Sukeforth's were filled constantly with sullen, hopeless bitterness. His son's eyes, on the other hand, were lit with a perpetual, smoldering rage that occasionally blazed into something bordering on madness.

'All right, Sukeforth,' Jed said. 'You found me.'

'I got word Brewster's planning on paying me a visit tomorrow, sheriff,' Sukeforth said plaintively.

'You mean you didn't expect that? You know damned well you're trying to claim land that he says belongs to him.'

'That's public land, sheriff,' said Will, his narrow face flaming righteously. 'You know that. So does Harlow Brewster. We ain't done nothin' wrong.'

Jed sighed, pushed his chair back, and got slowly to his feet. He had expected this, despite Brewster's promise to him earlier in the spring that he would let the courts decide. But he couldn't really blame Harlow Brewster. Sukeforth was pushing him into a corner by claiming a homestead on North Basin land.

'What do you want me to do, Sukeforth?' Jed asked. 'There's no laws says a man can't visit his neighbor, is there? Even if he is a squatter.'

Sukeforth ignored the quiet, appreciative laughter Jed's comment provoked. 'You know what I want, Sheriff.'

Jed nodded soberly. 'Protection.'

'You're a lawman. That's just what I want—and have a right to demand!'

Jed started past the two men. 'This ain't no place to discuss your private affairs, Sukeforth. We'd better continue this in my office.'

'No,' said Will. 'Let the whole town know what that rancher is up to. Let the citizens see what kind of sheriff they've got.'

Jed swallowed his anger. 'Suit yourself,' he said. 'Either you continue this discussion in my office or it ends here.' As he spoke he brushed past Will, heading for the batwings.

Abruptly, Jed felt Will Sukeforth's wiry hand closing about his arm. The strength in the man's fingers was surprising; before Jed could react, Will had flung him back and around with such force that Jed's back slammed painfully against the bar. For a moment his boots got tangled in the bar rail. Then he pushed himself away from the bar, ducked close in to Will, and drove his left fist deep into the man's gut. Will's reedlike body folded down just as Jed brought up his right fist, catching the young man flush on the point of his jaw. Will's head snapped back. Jed caught a glimpse of his wide-open, glazed eyes as Will went spinning onto a table. The

16

table collapsed under his weight and sent him sprawling heavily onto the floor. Groaning slightly, Will began to push himself through the muddy sawdust.

Sukeforth started to rush Jed in retaliation, but two of the men Jed had been playing poker with grabbed him from behind and held him by the elbows. At once Sukeforth gave up. The two men let him go, and the nester dropped to his knees beside his dazed son. Gently, carefully, working his jaw with his right hand, Will let his father help him to his feet. The man had been thoroughly beaten and the venom he had carried with him into the saloon not too long before seemed to have been drained out of Will for now, but the wild light in his eyes was enough to give Jed pause.

'Don't do that again, Will,' said Jed carefully. 'If you lay a hand on me one more time, be prepared for a lot worse than you just got.'

'The next time I lay my hands on you, Sheriff,' Will said, his voice trembling with icy rage, 'I'll make sure you can't move again. You'll be dead.'

'Shut up, Will!' Sukeforth cried. 'That's no talk from a son of mine! You think he's gonna help us now!'

'He wouldn't've helped us anyway, Pa! You know damned well Harlow Brewster owns him—lock, stock, and barrel!'

17

Jed's patience was long gone. Turning his back on the two, he rasped, 'Get out of here, both of you.'

Jed did not turn around as they slouched from the saloon. Hurriedly, the barkeep produced a bottle of Jed's favorite Maryland rye and poured him a stiff shot. As the batwings flipped shut behind Sukeforth and his son, Jed raised his glass to the barkeep and then, turning, to the men crowding around him. He smiled sardonically.

'Well, fellows,' he said, 'here's to Harlow Brewster and the Lazy 8. Looks like there's going to be some dust stirred up around here—and I'll be smack in the middle of it.'

There were solemn nods of agreement from the grim crowd as Jed downed the rye and turned back to the barkeep for a refill.

★   ★   ★

Jed left Sundown early the next morning. During the long ride out to Harlow Brewster's spread, he had plenty of time to review the events that were now forcing him into this lonely, early morning ride.

The problem was that Jed understood perfectly Harlow Brewster's dilemma. Like most everyone else in Sundown, he sympathized with the beleaguered cattleman. The Lazy 8's owner really had few, if any, options in this struggle of his with the

18

nesters. If he let Sukeforth take root in the North Basin, the rest of that nester's crowd would swarm in after him and start homesteading the land. The well-watered, lush grasslands that Brewster and the other three ranchers shared with him would be ripped up cruelly by the nesters' plows. Water holes and creeks would be fenced in; free movement of the herds across the basin would be impossible as traditional rights-of-way vanished.

Until three years before, there had been no dispute as to who owned the basin lands. But then, in a treaty trade with a Shoshoni tribe, the government had given the Indians land in the mountainous north in exchange for their lands in the North Basin. The new reservation line was the watershed of the Sawtooths, and all land south of that range was declared public land. At once, the North Basin's countless water holes and seeps and creeks, all of which made the land so valuable as cattle range, attracted the land hungry. A distant and indifferent Land Office held that, since the Shoshoni were not empowered to sell their land—as they had—to Brewster and the other ranchers, those purchases were invalid.

Nevertheless, Brewster and the others had petitioned the government for a hearing in Washington, and their plea had not fallen on deaf ears. And so the long court process of deciding who owned this land was under way. The problem now, as Brewster and the other ranchers saw it, was to prevent what might in fact become a *fait accompli*—homesteaders already settled in and farming the North Basin. The courts then would have no recourse. They would be forced by the pressure of public opinion to legitimize the nesters' claims. For agents of the federal government to be seen driving settlers from their homes would be unthinkable.

This was the game that Sukeforth was playing. It was a dangerous one and the stakes were high. Sukeforth was the opening wedge; if he could successfully call Brewster's bluff and settle in, the break in the dike would become a flood. It was up to Harlow Brewster then to call Sukeforth's bluff—to rid the North Basin of this intruder.

And it was up to Jed to see to it that things did not get out of hand—that no laws were broken, that neither the lives nor the property of those concerned in this deadly game were violated. The trouble was that Jed did not think very highly of his chances of achieving this. Harlow Brewster—as Jed had reason to know—was a man who made his own law since the day he settled here from Texas almost fifteen years ago.

★   ★   ★

The tangle of Lady 8 buildings, nestled in among a grove of giant cottonwoods, came in sight just before noon. A ranch dog picked Jed up and left a large barn to run toward him, yapping. A hand in a red-checked shirt came out after the dog and called him off. Jed rode through the gate into the compound, past the wagon sheds, then past the stables, heading for the big frame house. An old wrangler Jed recognized vaguely stepped out of the long log bunkhouse on his right and peered at him speculatively.

By the time Jed reached the main house, Harlow Brewster was standing on the low porch, his son Carl and his daughter Natalie beside him. Jed pulled up and touched the brim of his hat in greeting.

'Been expecting you,' Brewster said, his powerful face impassive. 'Almost left without you. But you're just in time.'

'For what?'

'You know the answer to that,' Brewster said. 'I heard Sukeforth was in Sundown yesterday, bellyachin'.' The man smiled thinly. 'I heard too that you and Will tangled some.'

'You heard right,' Jed acknowledged.

'Jed's probably had a long ride, Pa,' said Natalie. 'We don't have to set off right now. Clayt's still off rounding up the others.'

'Of course,' said Brewster. He looked coolly at Jed. 'Natalie's right, Sheriff. Light

21

and rest a spell. There's coffee in the kitchen.'

As Jed dismounted, Natalie said, 'I'll show him in, Pa. You and Carl can go see to your horses.'

★   ★   ★

The house was big and cool. The kitchen had plenty of windows and the sunlight blazed into it quite cheerfully. The stolid Indian housekeeper poured Jed his coffee and then left the room. Natalie poured herself a cup and sat down across from Jed at the broad, oaken table.

'You're not going to try to stop us, are you, Jed?'

'Is there anything on this earth big enough to stop your father?'

She replied, almost proudly, 'Not when he sets his mind to it.'

Jed sipped his coffee. 'That's what I figured.'

'Then why are you here?'

'To do what I can to prevent violence. I'm the law, don't forget.'

'There'll be no violence. This is just a show of force. Pa will give them twenty-four hours to leave—but he knows it'll take them longer than that. He promised me. He'll just ride up and surround the Sukeforths' place—give them a look at what's facing them.'

'And what's facing them Natalie?'

'Every rancher in the North Basin.'

'Every one?'

'Yes. That's where Clayt is now. He's gone to get riders from the Flying Seven, the Spur and the Barbed Y. Pa's uniting the whole basin against these squatters, and once Sukeforth and the others see that, they'll realize they can't possibly take our land from us.'

'You don't think so, Natalie?'

She bristled. 'We won't let them!'

Natalie was a woman in her early twenties, with black, lustrous hair and eyes just as dark. Her complexion was creamy and, like now, quick to register her emotions. Jed had always found her to be disturbingly beautiful. He knew she was aware of her effect on him. He had no doubt this was why she had invited him into the house, why she was sitting alone with him now at the kitchen table. She wanted him for an ally against the hated squatters and was not reluctant to use whatever charms she possessed to gain that allegiance.

She reached across the table and rested her hand on his forearm. Her eyes implored him, their shadowed depths glowing warmly. 'You understand, don't you, Jed? You know Pa and the rest of us have no alternative. This is our home, our land—and these ugly, dirty little squatters are trying to take it from us.'

23

Gently, Jed disengaged his arm from her grasp. 'I understand your problem, Natalie. I see how this could go, and I don't like it any more than you or your father does. But the law is the law.'

'They are trespassing!'

'Are they, Natalie?'

'You know they are!'

Jed sipped his coffee and shrugged. 'I suppose they are, at that. But it's just not as clear cut as you make it.'

'And why not?'

'This land you bought from the Shoshonis has been declared public land by the Land Office. Right now it's up to the courts to decide. But until they do—'

Natalie pulled herself back angrily. 'Jed! You mean that until the courts decide, you'll stand by Sukeforth! You'll fight Pa and all the rest of us! Is that it, Jed? Is that what you've decided?'

Calmly, Jed placed his coffee cup down on the table. 'Natalie,' he replied, 'the law doesn't take sides. I stand by any man who needs me. Your father—or Clyde Sukeforth. It's as simple as that.'

Natalie was on her feet, glaring down at him, her soft warmth of a moment before gone completely. Her dark eyes flashed angrily. 'I'm sorry, Jed. I thought we—the Lazy 8—stood for something in this land. And that you stood for the same thing.'

'My sympathies are with you and the rest of the ranchers. You know that, Natalie. But you must also know that I just cannot take sides, not while I'm the Sheriff. My only side is the law's side.'

'Lawyer's talk!' Natalie snapped. 'You're hiding behind that badge, Jed Sanford!'

The sound of heavy footsteps approaching the kitchen doorway caused both of them to turn. Harlow Brewster appeared in the doorway. Jed got to his feet. There was a question in Brewster's eyes. He had obviously heard his daughter's angry accusation. But before the man could question Natalie, she had stormed past him out of the kitchen.

The cattleman's tall frame appeared to sag momentarily as he looked at Jed. 'You told Natalie you're not with us. Is that it, Jed?'

'I told her I couldn't take sides.'

'Even after mixing it up with that crazy son of Sukeforth's?'

'That's right.'

'So Natalie figures if you ain't with us, you're against us.'

'That's what she thinks.'

Brewster was wearing a light, high-crowned Stetson and a long, gray broadcloth coat with tails. There was a bulge under it on one side caused by what Jed knew to be a holster containing a huge Navy Colt with walnut grips. Brewster's eyes peered at Jed out of deep, wide-set sockets, both his beetling eyebrows and his drooping moustache as white as the full head of hair that crowded out from under his Stetson's brim. He had a square, thrusting jaw and a voice that was powerfully resonant. There was nothing about his bearing that spoke of anything but strength—except, perhaps, for the slight limp that came, Brewster had once confided to Jed, from a shotgun wound he had sustained back in Texas many years before. The man's craggy face softened just a bit.

'Don't let Natalie buffalo you, Jed.'

'I won't.'

Brewster straightened and Jed saw the iron resolve reappear in his face. 'If you're coming with us, Sheriff, mount up. Clayt's brought the other riders and I've provided you with a fresh mount.'

Jed nodded his thanks. Brewster turned on his heel and led from the house, his stride still powerful, unyielding, except for the limp.

CHAPTER THREE

Clyde Sukeforth was frightened. His heart was an anvil sitting on his stomach. He had sent the women and the girls to North Fork Pass for safety and now waited with his son Will, Nathanial Tanner, and Zeke

Summerworth for Harlow Brewster to appear. Zeke had ridden in from the north a few minutes before with the word that Brewster's riders were kicking up a huge cloud of dust less than three miles away. Now Zeke, as nervous as Sukeforth, was standing in the open doorway with his Henry rifle, waiting.

Clyde was standing with his Winchester at the open window. Nate Tanner was outside in plain sight, striding up and down in front of the cabin, muttering to himself, his eyes wild, his long white patriarchal beard flowing behind him. He held an ancient Kentucky rifle in the crook of his right arm. Will was leaning back against a cottonwood tree near the stream, watching Nate. Occasionally Will would shout something to Tanner, and Sukeforth knew his son was goading the old minister, urging him to fulminate and carry on still more outrageously. Sukeforth felt the same way that his son did: Nathanial Tanner was half-mad. Still, Sukeforth had to admire the courage the man seemed to possess; it was his iron will that kept them all together against the ranchers. The man was a fiery, gifted orator. You might think him mad when he began to speak, but soon enough you fell under his spell and found yourself aroused and shouting in agreement before he was finished.

Well, thought Sukeforth glumly, it would

take more than words to turn back Harlow Brewster this day.

'They're here!' said Zeke from the doorway, stepping quickly out into the bright sunshine and looking south.

Sukeforth hurried out of the log cabin to see for himself.

Sukeforth's heart sank. Like Indians, Brewster's riders and all the others he had rounded up were spread along the ridge just a few hundred yards on the other side of the creek. They sat their horses as silent as death, peering down impassively at the four of them. There must have been thirty riders, all told—with Harlow Brewster, his whelps, the sheriff, and the three other owners the closest.

Beside him, Zeke said softly, 'Jesus.'

Will had hurried over to stand by his father, and Nathanial Tanner had simply stopped his agitated striding and now stood impassively, his rifle in his arms, his eyes seeming to flash out of his ancient, bronzed face.

'Say nothing!' Tanner commanded them. 'Let them speak first. Let them utter their own heartlessness! Let the sickness within their souls pour forth of its own volition!'

'Let me shoot that sonofabitching sheriff out of his saddle, Pa,' whispered Will, his eyes gleaming wolfishly. 'And then we can go for Carl. I hate that sonofabitch as much as

28

his old man.'

'No!' cried Sukeforth angrily, wincing at the venom he heard in his son's voice. Privation had done it, he told himself wildly. Not having, always being at the short end of every deal, hunger, bitterness—all of it had congealed in his young heart. And now he was unstrung. Sukeforth reached out and grasped his son by the arm. 'Stay with me, Will, Do as Nate says.'

'Tanner's a nut, Pa! He's looney!'

'Do as I say, Will.'

But Will pulled himself free of his father's grasp and moved a couple of feet closer to the line of horsemen facing them.

As Will did so, the riders, with Harlow Brewster in the lead, left the low ridge and rode down the short slope. In a moment their horses were splashing across the creek, and a second or two later the riders were spreading out in a circle, enclosing the small homestead, while Brewster and his party rode straight into the yard.

Brewster reined in first, his party pulling up alongside him, his daughter on one side, his son on the other, the Lazy 8 foreman and the sheriff to one side of the girl. The girl, Sukeforth noted, seemed as implacable as her father and was dressed in a black split riding skirt, black sombrero and vest. Her blouse under the vest was a flaming red. She might have been on her way to a fandango. The son

29

Carl had a cold smile on his face. A nest of vipers, Sukeforth thought, shuddering.

Though his mouth was sandpaper dry, he rasped out, 'Well, you're here, Brewster. You and your gang. Now what are you going to do? Shoot us down? Go ahead! But I warn you! We're armed. And we'll take some of you with us if we have to!'

'You've got more courage than brains, Sukeforth,' Brewster admitted. 'But I'm not looking for gunplay. I just want you to take your things and move out—back to North Fork Pass where the rest of your crowd is waiting, I understand.'

'We're not going anywhere, Brewster,' Will snapped.

At that moment the owners of the other ranches left their men, put their mounts across the creek and rode up to join Brewster. Nate Tanner took that moment to cross between Sukeforth and Brewster and stand boldly before the Lazy 8 owner, his feet wide apart, his ancient rifle cradled across his waist, his long white beard blowing wildly in the wind off the ridge.

Pointing to Yank Walsh of the Barbed Y, Tanner thundered, 'I know you, Walsh! You are a God-fearing Christian! It is a blot on your humanity that you ride with these legions of the devil!'

The broad-beamed, easy-going rancher looked uneasily over at Brewster. The man

30

was obviously distinctly uncomfortable at having been singled out by Nate Tanner. He moved his big frame forward on his saddle, causing the good leather in it to squeak. 'Aw, hell, Tanner! You got no call to go on like that! We ain't no devil's legions. We just don't want you people ruining our land is all.'

'So you would descend on us like barbarians! Is that it?'

Sandy Flynn of the Flying Seven took his hat off and rubbed his pink forehead with his bandanna. His light, reddish hair pulled in the stiff breeze. Then he clapped his hat back on and glanced at Brewster.

'How long we gonna sit here in this heat, Harlow? Ain't it about time we got to doin' what we rode out here to see done?' Walsh glanced at his companion, Pete Antell of the Spur. 'Ain't that what we rode here for, Pete? To run these nesters off?'

'It sure as hell is,' said Pete, bobbing his narrow face quickly. His watery blue eyes fixed on Sukeforth's face as he spoke.

Sukeforth took a deep breath and stepped forward to place himself alongside Tanner. He was astonished that his knees did not give way. He was aware of Will moving up beside him and he was enormously grateful. A moment later Zeke joined them.

Without warning Carl Brewster's gun was in his right hand. It exploded and a bullet ate dirt at Sukeforth's feet. It exploded a second time and Will's hat went flying off his head. As Will staggered back, slapping frantically at his now bared head in a futile effort to retrieve his hat, a roar of laughter erupted from the mounted riders that encircled them.

Tanner brought his rifle up. In that instant every rider drew his own six-gun. The sound of them all cocking their hammers sent a chill through Sukeforth. He reached over quickly and pushed Tanner's rifle down. The old man struggled. As the barrel swung down, the rifle went off. A bullet struck the ground just in front of Natalie Brewster's big chestnut. The animal reared. For a moment it appeared the girl would be unable to remain in the saddle. Fortunately, she was an expert rider and was able to gentle the horse down and stay in the saddle. But the sight of her fighting to control the horse infuriated her brother. Carl leaped from his horse and came at Sukeforth, his six-gun out.

When he raised it above his head, Sukeforth backed up hastily and flung up his arm to ward off the blow. But Carl crunched past Sukeforth's feeble defense and struck Sukeforth on the side of the head, a glancing blow that hurt cruelly and caused Sukeforth to stumble back. He saw Will fling himself on Carl. Instantly the two men were rolling in the dirt, pummeling each other.

Sheriff Sanford took that moment to put his horse between Harlow Brewster and

Sukeforth and then dismount. He reached down and yanked Carl Brewster off Will. When Carl tried to pull himself free of Jed, the sheriff simply pulled harder and sent Carl flying backward.

Then the sheriff looked up at the still mounted Harlow Brewster.

'So far,' the lawman drawled, 'we've all been pretty lucky. A few bloody noses and a spooked horse and maybe some bumps on the head. Now call off your men, Harlow. You delivered your warning. Sukeforth knows he's not welcome. So back off! Give him a chance to think this over!'

'No!' thundered Brewster. 'There's no sense drawing this quarrel out any longer! I want Sukeforth off this land. And I want him off now!'

Brewster's vehemence disheartened Sukeforth. His heart sank. He had a sense that it was going very badly despite Nate's assurance that God would not abandon them in this matter. Events seemed to have gotten out of hand. Even as this thought crossed his mind, he felt a crushing blow to the back of his head.

His knees sagged under him. He caught sight of Carl Brewster stepping past him and sticking the barrel of his six-gun into the sheriff's back. The man uttered a surprised grunt as he raised his hands over his head.

'You must be crazy, Carl,' he said.

'Shut up,' Carl replied, as he took the sheriff's gun from his holster.

With a cry of fury, Will flung himself once again on Carl. But this time Brewster's son clubbed Will viciously in the face. Will sagged crookedly to the ground. On his knees, still barely conscious from the blow on the back of his head, Sukeforth tried to reach out, tried to stop Carl from hurting his son. But all the wires were down. He saw Carl step back and fire with cold deliberation down at Will. Sukeforth heard himself crying out as he folded forward into darkness...

★   ★   ★

Harlow Brewster was proud of Natalie. Through it all she had remained calm. There was not, he realized now, a squeamish bone in her body. Plainly, she hated these nesters just as thoroughly as he did and understood perfectly what had to be done. And Carl, too. For the first time in a long time, Harlow was willing to believe that his son was ready now to take some responsibility for the Lazy 8. Perhaps gambling and town whores were not his only interest in life after all.

Clayt Durant galloped back across the creek and headed up the embankment toward them. The Lazy 8 foreman had a grim look on his face. As he pulled his horse to a stop beside Brewster, he could not refrain from glancing at Natalie.

'Sukeforth's kid is going to be all right,' Clayt told the cattleman.

'What about Sukeforth?' Natalie asked coldly.

'Same with him, Miss Natalie. Carl banged him up some. He's got a mean bump on the back of his head, but it's nothing serious. He'll just have to put his hat on careful for a while is all.'

'Where was Sukeforth's kid hit?' Brewster asked.

'In the shoulder. Just a flesh wound. Carl didn't aim to hurt him much.' He grinned. 'Just slow him down some.'

Brewster nodded and glanced down the trail beyond the burning buildings. Sukeforth was in sight driving a spring wagon piled high with gear and what few sticks of furniture the men had been able to pull from the log house before torching it. The preacher, Summerworth, and Sukeforth's son were crowded alongside Sukeforth on the plank seat. Two pathetically bony cows plodded along behind the wagon. A sorry procession, Brewster reflected, but one the nester had brought on himself.

Glancing back at the burning buildings, Brewster felt a vague unease, especially when he caught sight of Jed Sanford sitting his horse on the other side of the creek, staring moodily at the crackling ruins of the log

35

house. The flames were licking with patient enthusiasm at what remained of the roof after it collapsed a few moments before into the seething heart of the fire. The small barn and the outhouse had gone more quickly and were now only smoldering ashes.

Brewster glanced back at Clayt. In doing so, he thought he caught the gleam of a single tear on his daughter's cheek. He thought it best to ignore it as he addressed his foreman. 'How's the sheriff taking this?'

Clayt smiled ruefully. 'He's fit to be tied, Harlow.'

'Maybe I better have a word with him. You stay here with Natalie.'

Clayt seemed perfectly willing to do that.

Brewster put his horse down the embankment. As he splashed across the shallow creek, Jed turned his head. When the sheriff saw it was Brewster, he brought his horse around, his face turning cold.

'I suppose you're proud of yourself, Brewster,' Jed snapped.

'Doing what you have to do isn't always easy, Jed. But that sure as hell doesn't mean it shouldn't be done.'

Jed nodded, as if he had expected that response. Then he glanced bleakly, significantly around him. Brewster had sent the rest of the ranchers back, their riders with them. In a moment he would send his own riders back to the Lazy 8, as soon as Carl

36

returned. Carl had decided to ride a ways with Yank Walsh of the Barbed Y. The rancher had been pretty upset by the violence, and Carl had thought he had better see what he could do to settle the man down. The business was finished. The North Basin was safe—for now. Brewster caught the sullen resignation in Jed's eyes.

'I hope you're not thinking of pressing any charges, Sheriff.'

Jed snorted derisively. 'Carl and I will meet again soon enough, Harlow. And I don't suppose Sukeforth will be pressing any. You've got him pretty well terrorized, I'd say.'

Brewster nodded grimly. 'That was the idea. Besides, it would just be my witnesses against his, as well as your word against mine. Hell! Any responsible judge would only throw it out of court. You did what you could, Jed, and I respect you for it. I did what I had to do. That's the long and short of it.'

'Only I don't respect you for it, Brewster,' Jed said coldly. 'Not one bit.'

'Suit yourself,' Brewster replied.

'I will, Brewster. You can count on it.'

'Just don't forget who it was put you behind that badge, that's all. It was my friends on the council—and those ranchers you saw standing with me this afternoon.'

'That,' said Jed, pulling his horse around

and starting back along the creek, 'is something I can't forget, Brewster. No matter how hard I try.'

Brewster watched the sheriff ride off and was about to call out to him, reminding him that he was aboard Lazy 8 horseflesh. Then he thought better of it, turned his horse around, and spurred the animal back across the creek and up onto the embankment where Clayt and Natalie were waiting.

'Jed's angry, isn't he,' said Natalie, watching Jed lift his horse to a lope.

'And insubordinate.'

'He'll calm down. He's on our side, Pa. You know that.'

'I'm not so sure. You couldn't talk any sense into him back at the ranch, and he wasn't at all friendly just now.'

'Is he going to press charges against any of us?' Clayt asked.

Brewster shook his head. 'No. But that don't mean we won't have to walk soft around him from now on.' Brewster turned in his saddle and watched the disappearing horseman. 'I don't like it. Not one bit.'

The sound of an oncoming horse brought all three of them around. It was Carl. As he rode closer, the smile on his face meant only one thing to Brewster. Carl was heading into town to celebrate his day's accomplishments.

'Did you manage to calm Yank down?' Brewster asked his son.

38

'Sure,' Carl said, pulling his horse alongside Brewster. 'Only I ain't saying he won't unwind later. He's a real nervous Nellie.'

'I'll visit him and smooth things over myself tomorrow.'

Carl nodded absently. He was looking around for someone. Then he glanced at Brewster. 'Where's the sheriff?' There was a reckless smile on his face.

'He's gone back to town. He's not going to press charges, Carl, but it looks like all of us might better be more careful around him from now on.'

'Sure, I'll be careful.'

'I mean it, Carl. It's going to take a while for Jed to get himself to live with what happened here this afternoon.'

Carl shrugged. 'Hell. I'll give him all the time he needs. Just so long as he doesn't go out of his way to give me any trouble tonight.'

'Tonight?'

'Sure. I'm goin' into Sundown. I figure I got some celebratin' to do.' He looked at his sister, his eyes gleaming. 'Too bad you can't cut *your* wolf loose once in a while, Natalie.'

'I don't think you should go into Sundown tonight,' said Brewster.

Carl looked at his father. For a moment Brewster saw the face of his long-dead wife staring back at him from his son's countenance. It was in his eyes, of course.

39

The devilish mischief that had made her so attractive to him. Only in Carl it had an extra dimension, a dangerously reckless dimension. Something wild, fugitive, lived in Carl. Whatever it was, he didn't like it, for it was this elusive instability that acted as a barrier between him and his son. There was something hidden in Carl that caused this, he knew. And what it was Brewster was almost afraid to discover.

'Why not?' Carl asked. 'Ain't I deserved a little relaxation.'

'I just figure it would be a good idea if you didn't let your wolf loose tonight, while Jed's still so skittish about what happened today. Give the man room, Carl.'

'You think he could take me?'

'He's never had much trouble, has he?'

Carl's face darkened.

'Damn it, Carl. That ain't the point. Jed's the sheriff. He's *our* sheriff. We put him there. It's hard enough for him to stand still for what happened today without you going into town tonight and pouring salt into his wounds by letting everyone know what happened out here.'

'You think everyone in Sundown won't know anyway?'

Brewster sighed. 'I'm sure they will, Carl. But you just might be the last straw for Jed.'

'Yeah,' Carl replied, smiling quickly. 'I just might.'

40

The coldness in the smile—the eager meanness of it—alarmed Brewster. 'Carl, I want you to ride over to North Fork Pass and see what the rest of these nesters are up to. That's where I understand this fellow Tanner is organizing these settlers, charging them up. You heard him today. He's a preacher, filled with fire and brimstone, and he's the one been goading the rest of them into squatting on North Basin land. I think you ought to ride over there and have a look around.'

'Not tonight, Pa. Tomorrow.'

His son's defiance was so casual that it took Brewster completely by surprise. It was as if the man had crossed a barrier this day that released him from any further obligation to do as he was told.

'You do as I say, Carl, or pack your roll and get off Lazy 8 land.'

'I'm just one more cowpoke, is that it?' Carl asked, evenly, his face suddenly drawn.

'Carl!' Natalie cried, looking at the two of them anxiously. 'You know better than that! Why can't you do as Pa says?'

'Stay out of this, Natalie,' Brewster said carefully. 'This is between your brother and me.' He glanced back at his son, a coldness closing about his heart as he saw the implacable hostility in Carl's eyes. 'You haven't been much of a cowhand, Carl. Town whores and gambling have been your occupations. If it weren't for Natalie and

41

Clayt, I'd have been pretty much on my own running the Lazy 8. If you want to be more than just another cowpoke on the Lazy 8, you'll have to begin to pull your own weight.'

'I thought I just did that,' Carl said tightly.

'There's more to ranching than slugging a nester from behind and shooting his unarmed son.'

'Is there, Pa?' Carl leaned forward in his saddle and stared insolently into his father's eyes. 'Why, hell! All this time I been thinking that's all there was to it! Now what do you think of that! I guess I must've had it all wrong.'

Brewster sat back in his saddle, his anger on a very tight rein. 'You going over to North Fork Pass?'

'Nope. And I'm not packing my bedroll, either.'

Clayt cleared his throat. 'I'll ride over to the North Fork, Harlow,' the foreman said. 'Won't take me long. Be back by sundown. Wanted to check out our line shack, anyways. Slim said the roof's in bad shape.'

'Now there, you see? Good ole Clayt'll be glad to check out them nesters,' Carl said. 'Yessir! Bet you wouldn't want ole Clayt to pack his bedroll, would you.'

The venom in Carl's tone dismayed Brewster. From the look on Clayt's and Natalie's faces, Brewster could tell that they were just as surprised. Brewster wanted no

42

more of this. He turned to Clayt.

'All right,' he told his foreman. 'I want to know how many outfits they've got there, and maybe some idea of what they might be planning once Sukeforth and Tanner tells them what happened here. I'd like it if they started packing and moved on. There's a chance this day's business might convince all of them to pull out.'

Clayt nodded.

'I'll go with him, Pa,' said Natalie.

When Brewster saw the way Clayt's face brightened at the prospect, he decided not to argue—even though he was not entirely pleased at the prospect of Natalie and his foreman riding off together. 'All right, Natalie,' he said, aware of a sudden, almost overwhelming weariness settling over him. After all, at one time nothing would have pleased him more than to see Natalie show an interest in Clayt.

Carl sat his horse impassively and said not a word as Natalie and Clayt turned their horses about and rode off toward the dim jumble of peaks in the west. When they were out of earshot, he looked coldly at his father.

'Make a nice pair, don't they?' he said.

Brewster frowned. 'What's that got to do with anything. You refused to go, so Clayt's going. And you know Natalie. She's one hell of a lot more interested in this ranch than you are.'

43

'Is she now?'

'That's the way it looks to me.'

'And Clayt. He's interested too, ain't he.'

'This is pointless, Carl. I'm tired. You want to argue, we'll do it later. The men are all watching us, and I've got to get back to the ranch. If you're going to Sundown, go on.'

'I'll do just that, Pa. But before I go, I want to remind you of something.'

'And what's that?'

'I'm your son. Your firstborn son.'

'I know that.'

'Your son and *heir*.'

'You make it sound like a curse.'

Carl smiled icily at his father. 'Maybe it is.'

Carl hauled his horse around suddenly, brutally, and lifted it to a swift canter as he headed across the grassland toward Sundown. Watching him ride, Harlow Brewster felt a deep uneasiness—a sense of foreboding so strong he could taste it. He forced it resolutely from himself, turned his horse, and rode toward his men, who were already mounted and waiting for him beyond the ridge.

CHAPTER FOUR

Natalie asked Clayt for the binoculars. Clayt handed them to her. She held them up to her

44

eyes and adjusted them quickly.

As the wagons and tents locked into focus and she caught sight of the children playing about the hastily constructed shanties and sod houses, Natalie could not help feeling a pang of guilt. She had felt the same way earlier, when she had watched Sukeforth drive off in his wagon, those two skeletal cows following after. She resolutely fought back the guilt and told herself that these families below her in the pass were bent on destroying the Lazy 8 and everything her father and mother had struggled to build.

A little girl with long golden pigtails fell suddenly, and as Natalie kept the binoculars on her, she saw a dirty-faced, towheaded boy a few years older than the girl reach down, snatch one of her shoes off her foot, and run off, holding the single shoe aloft. The little girl began to cry, her face twisting into silent grief, and Natalie immediately looked away and handed the binoculars back to Clayt.

'Here,' she said. 'I've seen enough.'

Clayt took the binoculars and nodded. 'There sure are a lot of families down there—just waitin' to squat on North Basin land. It's a damned good thing we sent them Sukeforths packin'.'

Natalie nodded. They had followed the Sukeforths at a distance and were now inside the line shack overlooking the pass. Sukeforth had been greeted warmly by his wife and daughter, but it was obvious from the reception he got how disheartened they were to see him enter the settlement. For a while that preacher, Tanner, had gathered them all about him and had harangued them; but it didn't take long for the families to drift off to their separate shacks and tents, leaving Tanner alone beside a patched and poorly set up tent. Clayt was right. Her Pa's actions this afternoon, brutal though they were, had saved the Lazy 8 and the other ranchers from this hive of swarming settlers.

'I agree, Clayt,' she told the foreman. 'I just wish Sukeforth could have left without our having to burn his place, that's all.'

Clayt smiled at her. 'You're an old softie,' he told her. 'You always were. I remember you used to bring in baby woodchucks to feed if you found them without their mama. You ain't like Carl. You'll do what has to be done, but that don't mean you're going to like it. I could see how you felt when we were settin' fire to that squatter's place.'

'You noticed, did you?' Natalie asked, surprised suddenly at the way Clayt was looking at her. His eyes were shining, almost in adoration of her.

'I've been noticing you for a long time, Natalie.' Clayt's voice was husky.

'I'm sure you have,' Natalie said, a sudden confusion falling over her. 'I've been noticing you, too. You've done a fine job for Pa these past four years. With Carl off to town most every day, you've been a great help. I'm sure Pa appreciates it.'

'The thing is, Natalie, I want *you* to appreciate it.'

'Well, certainly, Clayt. I appreciate it.'

'Is that all, Natalie?'

'What do you mean?'

'I mean, is that all you feel? Just appreciation.'

'What more do you want me to feel, Clayt?'

'Don't you know?'

Oh, God! Of course she knew. That was the problem. She knew only too well what Clayt was driving at; and she cursed herself for allowing the conversation to take this unfortunate turn. 'Clayt,' she said tentatively, aware that her face was flaming with embarrassment, 'of course I know. But now . . . is not the time or the place for this kind of a discussion.'

Clayt took a quick stride toward her and placed both hands on her shoulders. His lean, honest, cowpuncher's face was flushed with emotion, his pale blue eyes searching her face desperately for some sign that she felt as he did. 'Yes, this is the time!' he cried anxiously. 'We'll never have a better time!'

'Oh?' Natalie shrugged off his hands and took a step back into the shadows of the line shack. 'Really, Clayt. This is *not* the time *or* the place for a discussion of our feelings.

Don't you think we should be getting back now? We've seen enough here.'

'What's the matter, Natalie?' He followed after her, coming to a halt with the light from the open window flooding over him.

Natalie saw the tight anger in his lean face. But now she was angry, too. Clayt was, after all, only her father's hired hand. Of late, Clayt had been acting as if he, not Carl, was the heir apparent to the Lazy 8. And perhaps her father *had* toyed with the idea that she might marry Clayt and take over the ranch if Carl did not settle down. But she was certainly not ready for such a move at this moment.

And now that she thought of it, she didn't think she would ever find herself willing to marry this well-meaning, but essentially unexciting, top hand. No matter how greedy he was for her—and for what she could bring to him as his bride.

Abruptly, Clayt reached out, took her in his arms and pulled her clumsily toward him. He tried to kiss her on the mouth. Natalie turned her face aside as she pushed frantically against his chest. He only clasped her more tightly against him, and this time his lips found her neck, and then her hair. Her fury gave her the strength she needed, and she twisted wildly out of his arms. Once she was far enough away, she brought up her right hand and slapped him in the face. It was a blistering crack that sent Clayt back a few steps, his right hand up to his cheek, tears of rage and pain gleaming in his wide, furious eyes.

'You deserved that, Clayt!' Natalie said, aware that her heart was thumping furiously against her breast bone, like a wild animal, caged. Her breath came in short, rasping gasps. 'How *dare* you!'

'There's something the matter with me, isn't there, Natalie,' Clayt said, his voice low and filled with an edged nastiness that caused Natalie to shudder inwardly. 'I'm not good enough for you, that's what's the matter. I'm just your father's hired hand. That's all I am to you. Isn't that right?'

'Yes!' snapped Natalie brutally. 'That *is* all you are. My father's hired hand. A top hand. A good foreman. But that's all, Clayt. And I never gave you leave to think anything different.'

'And I'm finished now. Is that it?'

'Yes! You're finished at the Lazy 8. And when my father hears what happened here, you'll be lucky to leave with your bedroll intact!'

'Well, then,' said Clayt grimly, 'it looks like I might just as well take as much as I can while I'm at it.'

Clayt took a slow, menacing step toward her. Natalie backed up, sudden fear washing over her. And then she felt the damp long

49

wall against her back. 'Get away from me, Clayt. I warn you!'

'Go ahead! Scream. Do you think those settlers down there will come to your aid? Do you think they'll even hear you?'

'I'll not scream. I'll not let them know I was foolish enough to trust you—and was then spineless enough to scream for help.' She straightened and stepped away from the wall, proudly, almost regally. 'And you'll not touch me, Clayt Durant! You know what would happen to you if you did.'

'Good,' Clayt said, reaching out and cupping her out-thrust jaw in his hand. 'That's fine. I'm glad you won't scream. But I *am* going to touch you, my proud lady. I been waiting too long to let this opportunity pass. And sure I know what will happen if I do. Your father will send riders after me.' He chuckled softly at the thought. 'I know those men. I can outride and outshoot every single one of them. They don't scare me none—and neither does your old man.'

Natalie moved closer to Clayt, her eyes softening, the angry line of her mouth lifting in what was the hint of a smile. 'All right, damn you,' she breathed, moving into his arms. 'Do it and get it over with. Take what you want, then ride out.' She looked up into his face and tipped hers slightly, waiting for his response.

Smiling bitterly, he pulled her roughly

50

closer and bending his face over hers, caught her lips with his own in a harsh, devouring kiss. She answered his kiss with a surprisingly ferocious passion and pressed against him so urgently that he found himself taking an involuntary step backward. Her left hand flashed down, caught the butt of his six-gun, and lifted it free just as Clayt regained his balance. She stepped quickly back and away from him. Stunned at the suddenness of her tactic, he could only stare, dumbfounded, as Natalie swiftly, expertly, slipped the gun into her right hand and leveled it at him. In the dark cabin he saw the light of triumph gleaming in her eyes.

'Now, you sonofabitch!' she breathed, panting in her fury. 'Maybe my father don't scare you, and maybe you *can* outride and outshoot any riders he sends after you. But you can't outshoot me now, not while I got your weapon!'

'Natalie!'

'Back up, damn you!'

'Natalie! Please! Be careful with that gun!'

'Why? If it goes off, I'll just tell my father what happened. He'll be quite proud of me, I should think!'

Clayt seemed beside himself with fear. He held his hand out, as if to ward off the bullets he felt sure would soon be poured in his direction. Natalie thought for a moment he was going to collapse onto the dirt floor on his

51

knees. She stepped closer to him, leaning her face angrily forward.

'I said get back,' she told him. 'I want you out of here this instant!'

Clayt seemed about to move back, his eyes pleading with her in the dark room. She felt enormous contempt for him now and took another step closer. Clayt's hand lashed out, caught the barrel of his six-gun, and yanked it from her grasp. It thudded to the floor of the line shack and before Natalie could dive for it, he had grabbed both her wrists and pulled her cruelly toward him, a triumphant smile on his face.

'You have to cock a single shot before you can fire it, Natalie!' he told her, sweeping an arm about her. 'And now this time you really *are* going to deliver!'

'No!' Natalie began to struggle.

He laughed, stepped back, and slapped her on the side of the face with his one free hand, while his other still held her right wrist. Then he backhanded her, the brutal force of it snapping her face back around, after which he yanked her close a second time.

'Be nice,' he told her harshly. 'This ain't gonna hurt, unless you want it that way! Figure it's an Indian raid. Lean back and make the most of it.'

She stopped struggling. He saw the tears of rage gleaming on her cheeks in the late afternoon sun filtering in through the two windows and the open door. 'Please,' she said. 'Not here. Not in this damp, ugly place.'

He relaxed and looked quickly about him. At once she pulled away from him. He caught at her and grabbed her shirt and vest. She spun angrily around, the shirt tearing loudly in the dark place. But then she was free. She flung herself to the floor and reached out for the gleaming revolver where it lay in a patch of light streaming in through the open doorway. As her hand closed about the butt, Clayt kicked her in the side and sent her tumbling across the dirt floor. But as she rolled, she clung to Clayt's revolver and managed to cock it—as he had reminded her to do. Clayt started swiftly, angrily, toward her, bent like some prowling beast. Coming to a halt, she aimed the revolver with both hands and fired.

She heard the bullet hit him, saw Clayt halt his charge. But he didn't go down. She cocked again and fired. This second slug's impact spun Clayt completely around, driving him back into the shadows beyond the door. This time he fell, the sound of his heavy body striking the dirt floor sickening her. To her horror, he turned about and began to crawl toward her.

Snatching up her sombrero, she scrambled to her feet, dropped Clayt's revolver, and darted from the shack. When she reached the pines where they had tethered their horses, she heard Clayt fire at her from the shack. How could he still be alive? she thought bitterly, as she stepped blindly into her saddle, hauled her horse around, and galloped recklessly back through the timber, her head down, angry tears streaking her face.

★　　★　　★

By the time the echo of the fourth shot had joined the first three, Clyde Sukeforth had snatched up his Winchester and hurried from Tanner's tent with the bearded preacher close behind him, his eyes glaring up at the forested slope that hung above them. Will was the last one out, a purple welt down the left side of his face, his left arm resting in a fresh sling.

'God curse them!' Tanner cried, shaking his fist at the dim smudge he knew to be Lazy 8's line shack. The shots seemed to have come from there. 'You were right, Will. They followed us here!'

Sukeforth looked quickly about. A woman was frozen before a campfire. Children had halted their play. Grim men gazed up at the mountainside as the last echoes faded.

There was no sign anyone had been hit. And no whine of bullets had followed the gunfire. The shots had sounded muffled; the detonations did not have the clean crack of rifle fire. In the tense silence, Sukeforth turned to his son.

'I'm going up to that line shack to investigate, Will. I want you to stay here with Nate and take care of your mother and sister.'

Predictably, Will was disappointed. 'Pa!' he cried. 'You can't keep me down here! I'm going with you! How do you know how many there are up there? Ma and Sherry'll be safe down here. They ain't alone.'

'That shoulder wound will slow us, Will,' he said quietly. 'Besides, those shots might have been just a trick to draw us up to that ridge—while the rest of their crew circle around behind us. You and the others stay back here and keep a sharp lookout. Maybe it would be a good idea to send all the women and children into the cabin near the creek. Just in case.'

'I can still go with you, Pa.'

'No. You stay back here. I'll feel better if I know you and Tanner are watching for any tricks. Maybe Zeke and Matthew could go down the creek further. They might come that way.' He smiled wanly at Will. 'Don't worry. I'll keep my ass down.'

Will took a deep breath and nodded. 'Okay, Pa. We'll keep our eyes peeled down here. But if you need any help, just holler.'

'If you hear I've started a war up there, come runnin'. Don't wait for my holler. Just come.'

Will nodded. Sukeforth turned and started for the slope.

★   ★   ★

On his belly behind a clump of juniper, Sukeforth peered intently at the line shack. It was as silent as death. It looked like part of the roof had fallen in. Both windows and the door were open wide. Looking closer, Sukeforth saw that there were no window panes in the windows and the door was not open; it was missing entirely. There had been no more firing since he started up the mountainside. That didn't mean anything, of course. At any moment, he knew, firing might erupt behind him in the pass below.

Certain the line shack was empty, Sukeforth was about to start back down the mountainside when his eyes caught movement in the pines further up the slope. He froze and looked more closely. It was a horse. He saw its tail twitching. He saw the horse's head jerk up and back as the animal tried to pull free of the reins that held him. Sukeforth glanced back at the line shack. Nothing. Then the horse turned and vanished from sight behind a line of trees. The horse hadn't gone anywhere, he knew, just shifted his position in relation to the pines. That was why he hadn't seen the animal a moment before.

Sukeforth considered his options.

He could investigate the horse, look for footprints leading from it, search the area more thoroughly—or he could hurry back down to the others waiting below. He wanted to go back down to the pass. The smell of all this was bad, and his nerves were already shot from the day's bitter humiliations.

Sukeforth swore softly to himself.

He couldn't go back down and face his son without even investigating that horse. He could at least inspect the brand on it. That should tell him something. And besides, whoever it was had left the horse and was skulking around taking shots at them would have to return to the horse eventually.

And Sukeforth would be waiting. He could capture him.

The thought was unnerving to Sukeforth, but he bolstered his courage by imagining what it would be like to bring the sonofabitch down to the others. Will would like that. Tanner, too. And the woman and kids. They would all crowd around to confront their tormentor. Maybe it was Brewster's son—or Clayt Durant, the foreman.

Sukeforth's tongue darted out and licked his dry lips. He cleared his throat softly and took a deep breath, then looked down at his Winchester for assurance. He had long since levered a fresh round into the firing chamber. Taking another deep breath, he got slowly to

57

his feet, and keeping low, darted across the clearing toward the pines. In a moment he had glided through the trees to the side of the tethered horse. The Lazy 8 brand stood out brazenly on the big chestnut's rump.

As if there could have been any doubt, Sukeforth told himself, dropping to one knee and peering carefully around.

He would have to wait now. He didn't like the idea. He could be surprised by whoever it was. He glanced through the pines at the shack. Maybe he should wait in there out of sight. He would be able to see the Lazy 8 rider return for his horse. It was only a few yards from the pines. He wouldn't be able to surprise the sonofabitch as easily, but it would be a whole hell of a lot safer.

Sukeforth argued with himself no longer. Keeping low, he slipped through the pines and darted into the line shack.

CHAPTER FIVE

It was dusk when Natalie rode into the Lazy 8 compound. Instead of riding directly to the stables, she dismounted at the hitch rail in front of the main house, then hurried around to enter by the kitchen door.

Alice Lone Bear turned her massive figure as Natalie closed the kitchen door silently behind her. At once the Indian housekeeper saw Natalie's torn blouse and caught the distraught look on Natalie's face. Natalie brought her forefinger up to her mouth. Alice put down the mixing bowl she held and simply stared back at Natalie, her broad face impassive.

'Where's Pa?' Natalie asked softly.

'Outside.'

Natalie breathed a quick sigh of relief, shrugged out of her vest and swiftly unbuttoned the red, silken blouse. Handing it to Alice, she said, 'Wash it, then mend it.'

Alice took it from her. When she reached for the vest also, Natalie shook her head.

'No, the vest is all right. Tell no one, Alice. This is my business. Do you understand?'

Alice's black eyes gleamed with a sudden awareness. Perhaps her father had mentioned to the woman that Natalie had ridden off with Clayt.

'I'll be upstairs, in my room, getting out of these things. Has Pa been looking for me?'

'At supper, he asked about you.' The expression on Alice's face barely changed. 'I think he was some worried. But he said nothing. Shall I tell him you are home?'

'If he asks for me. But I want time . . . to freshen up.'

Alice folded the blouse. 'I put this away . . . now. After I wash it, I sew it for you.'

'Yes,' said Natalie starting from the

59

kitchen. 'I'd like it back as soon as you can manage, Alice.'

Natalie left the kitchen then and hurried up the stairs to her room. She lit the lantern on her dresser with shaking hands, then swiftly undressed. She kept her eyes averted from her nakedness. She felt ashamed of her body. As if it were that which had betrayed her. She had heard other women speak of this: the guilt they felt when any man tried to assault them. It was difficult not to believe that in some way they had brought it on themselves; and perhaps they had. After all, it was so damnably difficult to act always as if a man's hard hand on her own yielding flesh was not something desirable—even necessary. There were so many ways one's body could betray one. The flush of one's cheeks, the sudden intake of breath when they came too near. Yes, it was damnably difficult, and she should not have allowed Durant to get that close to her in the line shack. After all, she had known from the beginning how he felt about her . . .

She dressed in her long blue nightgown, buttoning it up to the neck and then tying the sash securely about her waist. Only then did she allow herself to look in the mirror. Her face, she saw, was still flushed, her eyes unnaturally bright. All that crying on the ride home, she realized. But though she looked as pure as the driven snow, she still felt unclean.

60

There was a soft rap on her door. She opened it. Alice Lone Bear was standing in the doorway, the bathtub in her arms. Natalie moved back into the room, suddenly grateful for the Indian woman's unerring instincts.

After Alice set the empty bathtub down on the floor between the dresser and the bed, she straightened and told Natalie that she had many kettles of water heating downstairs and that as soon as Natalie finished her bath, Alice would let Natalie's father up to see her. He was downstairs now. The man had entered the kitchen and asked for her—and for Clayt—as soon as he had discovered Natalie's horse at the tie rail in front of the house.

Natalie heard this as if she were listening from a great distance. She sat down on her bed and watched Alice leave, stunned. Slowly, mechanically, she unbuttoned her robe, more grateful each minute for the promised bath. She would need it to steam the filth from her. And it would give her time ... the time she desperately needed if she were going to be able to explain to her father what had happened.

But how could she? It was too ugly! She had wounded and probably killed a man who had attempted to rape her, the same man whom her father had trusted and loved almost as a son. At times, in his exasperation with Carl, she was certain her father had seriously

61

contemplated offering Clayt half-interest in the Lazy 8. Until recently, she knew, it would not have displeased her father if she and Clayt had become interested in each other . . .

She shuddered involuntarily at the thought.

The door opened and Alice entered ponderously, carrying two steaming kettles. Natalie snatched up the soap and a wash cloth Alice had left for her on the bed, stepped into the ornately flowered, high-backed tub, and leaned back as the impassive woman poured the steaming water over her sinful, wicked nakedness.

★   ★   ★

A good half hour later, a few minutes after Alice left her room with the tub, Natalie heard her father's anxious rap on her door. Natalie, sitting on the edge of her bed, rightened the sash of her robe and called out for her father to enter.

He pulled open the door and strode in, his lined face drawn. 'You all right, Natalie?' he asked, pulling the door shut and approaching the bed.

'Of course, Pa,' she replied, smiling.

He looked at her carefully, studying her face with his fiercely protective eyes. They seemed to blaze out at her, to be able to see into her very soul. 'You seem ... strange. I thought sure you'd be back for supper, you and Clayt. Where is he?'

'I got tired of spying on the settlers, but he seemed to like it. So I rode on back here and let him skulk around to his heart's content. Those people in the pass are a pitiful lot. I don't see that they're any longer a danger to us—not after today.'

'That's your assessment, is it?'

'Yes.'

'Well, I don't much like the idea of Clayt letting you ride back here alone. The land is filled with them crazy homesteaders. Nothing they'd like better than to take a pot shot at Harlow Brewster's daughter.' He looked at her still more closely than before. 'You didn't get into any kind of trouble, did you?'

'Trouble?'

'With the homesteaders.'

'I'd tell you, wouldn't I, Pa?'

'I don't know. I thought you handled yourself very well this afternoon. It was not a pleasant business, but you stood firmly by my side. I was proud of you. But later I saw a tear on your cheek. Perhaps it *was* too much for you, after all. Perhaps your sympathies are turning toward the nesters.'

'And so if they did something to me on the ride back to the Lazy 8, I wouldn't tell you? I would hide it from you?'

'Yes, Natalie. That's what I was thinking.'

'I came across no homesteaders during my ride home. But I did get pretty dirty after that ride. So I asked Alice to heat some water for a bath. And right now I am famished, Pa. It's been a long day.' She tried to smile. 'There's no reason for you to be so concerned about me. I'm a big girl now. Believe me. There's nothing wrong.'

He seemed relieved. Straightening, he smiled, 'Yes,' he said. 'You *are* a big girl. I just don't want anything to happen to you. That's all.'

Still smiling, she said, 'Well, something will happen to me if I don't get some food in me soon. I'll shrink away to nothing. Now you just get out of here while I dress. I'll be down in a few minutes.'

'Fine,' he said, heading for the door. 'I'll tell Alice.'

★　　　★　　　★

As soon as she heard the fading footsteps of her father on the stairs, Natalie flung herself down on the bed. The sobs that wrenched themselves from her throat she effectively muffled in the soft down of the bedspread. She let the torrent carry her for a while until, exhausted, she began to wipe her eyes. At last she sat up and looked bleakly around her, an occasional dry sob breaking from her.

Then she dressed herself in her dark

peasant blouse and split riding skirt, only dimly aware that what she was putting on was not entirely appropriate for this time of day. But she paid no attention. Slipping on her leather high-heeled boots, she stood up and caught a glimpse of herself in her dresser mirror. Her hair needed combing.

She sat down at her vanity, pulled a dusty bottle of brandy from a bottom drawer, carefully poured some of it into an equally dusty shot glass, placed the shot glass beside her on the vanity, stoppered the bottle, and placed it back in the drawer. Then she picked up her brush and began combing out her dark hair. She could still feel Clayt's claw-like hands on her; she could still smell the man as he leaned close and tried to enclose her lips with his own. She combed with more rapid strokes as she stared at herself in the mirror and saw, not herself, but his body coming for her in the darkness of the line shack, then bucking and spinning as her bullets found him.

No. She would not reveal to anyone what that man subjected her to—and what she had done to him as a result. If he lived, he would not have the courage to admit his depravity to anyone. If he died ... let them wonder who killed him. Let his body rot for all she cared ...

She was still combing her hair a half hour later, her strokes methodical, her eyes peering with an almost demented intensity at the image of herself in the mirror, when Alice Lone Bear knocked softly on her bedroom door and entered.

Alice said not a word to Natalie about the empty shot glass on the vanity, gently disengaged the brush from Natalie's hand, and speaking to her softly, reminded her that supper was waiting for her downstairs.

Like someone wrenching herself from a dream—or more accurately, a nightmare— Natalie stirred herself, closed her eyes for a moment, then stood up and left the room with the housekeeper.

★   ★   ★

Jed was eager to purge the disquiet that clung to him, the nagging sense of his own helplessness in the face of events, as he mounted the unsteady porch that fronted Jenny's place, knocked once on the kitchen door, and let himself in. The room was lit by two lanterns, one on the deal table and the other on the sideboard near the doorway that led into the small living room. A pot of coffee was simmering on the stove. Jed smiled when he saw it; Jenny had evidently expected him.

He called her name once, loudly, then slumped wearily into a chair by the table. He had arrived back in Sundown well before nightfall, but he had spent the entire evening, it seemed, settling squabbles in the various saloons. There was an edginess in the air of the town that boded no good, a sense of impending violence. Even a couple of his poker buddies had seemed cold and unfriendly when he passed them in the street. Of course Jed knew why. Since when did a Milk River County Sheriff try to protect nesters? Jed shook his head wearily. They really had little cause to complain. A fat lot of good Jed's protection had been that afternoon. The nesters had been brutally and thoroughly routed by Brewster's forces.

He sighed, took off his hat, and placed it down on the table beside him. Then he leaned back in his chair, ready to call out to Jenny a second time—when he saw Jenny and Carl entering the kitchen. There was a look of pain mixed with pity on Jenny's face, a hard look of triumph on Carl Brewster's.

Jed jumped to his feet, feeling as if he had just been kicked in his gut. And he had been. Jenny with Carl! Alone in there. His mouth as dry as sandpaper, he reached for his hat.

'No need to rush off, Sheriff,' Carl said easily, a broad smile on his face now. 'Jenny's got a pot of coffee heatin' over there on the stove. I'll join you.' He paused deliberately, cruelly. 'I'm all tuckered out.'

His meaning was unmistakable, and it was enough to give Jed the excuse he wanted. With a furious cry, he flung himself across

67

the room at Carl. His first looping blow caught Carl high on the head. Carl staggered back and came up heavily against the doorjamb. Jed was dimly aware of Jenny's slight hand on his arm. He shook it off angrily and backed up, waiting for Carl's response. Carl hesitated.

'Come on, Carl,' Jed taunted. 'I'm facing you this time. Shall I turn my back on you?'

Jenny, on the far side of the table by this time, her combed-out hair an explosion of darkness about her pale face, reached out a hand toward Jed. 'Don't, Jed!' she pleaded. 'Please!'

Carl charged suddenly to one side and snatched up a chair. Flinging it over his head, he rushed toward Jed. Jed saw the stark hatred Carl felt for him. It was mirrored in his twisted face as he flung the chair down and forward. Jed raised one arm and took the blow, and shunted the chair aside. He stepped on and drove a punch deep into Carl's left side, into the soft flesh just above the hip. He heard Carl's sharp, painful exhalation as Carl let the chair drop and flung himself furiously on Jed, both hands swinging. One of his fists struck Jed on the cheek, sending him back.

As he followed up this punch, Jed ducked low and staggered Carl with a blow to his midsection. Carl was flung back against the wall, his mouth springing open as he gasped for air. Moving in swiftly, Jed hit him slantingly on the mouth, drawing blood. He saw Carl's head snap around slackly. But somehow Carl remained upright. Jed measured carefully and hooked another side blow across Carl's face, catching him on the cheekbone. A light of fury exploded in Carl's eyes and he shook off the blows, lowered his head, and came at Jed again.

He took fearful punishment as he slammed in through Jed's punches and drove him back against the stove. Carl's wild, looping punches caught the coffee pot and sent it tumbling. Jed felt the sharp flare of pain on the backs of his legs as the hot coffee spilled down the back of his Levi's. He flung an arm around Carl's head and gave it a twist. Carl was flung to one side. He stumbled and tried to maintain his balance. Before he could right himself and face Jed, Jed drove his fist down on the back of the man's neck with all the force he could muster.

The blow caused Carl to sag to his knees. As Jed positioned himself in front of Carl, the rancher's son shook his head blearily and thrust both hands up to ward off Jed's next blow. Jed hit him on the mouth, following through so completely that his back was to Carl when he finished his swing. Carl went sprawling across the floor on his hands and knees, coming to a halt with his shoulder against the wall. He placed one hand on the wallpaper, then sagged slowly to the floor. When he came to rest he was spread-eagled, his face up, his eyes flickering, his bloodied mouth open wide.

He seemed to be trying to say something.

Jed turned away from him and found Jenny. She was standing in the far corner of the room, the one closest to the door.

As he started toward her, she uttered a tiny scream and held her arm up against her face. She was terrified of him. It was that fact that sobered him finally. And saddened him, as well. This woman he had loved so completely, so foolishly—this woman who had protested how much she loved him as she nibbled his ear lobes and murmured softly to him—this woman was now afraid of him. He pulled up and snatched his hat off the table.

'Thanks, Jenny,' he said tightly. 'Thanks a lot.'

'I promised you nothing! It was all you! You think because you take me from Rose and rent this dump for me that I'm yours! That you own me!'

'Did I ever say that?'

'Damnit! It ain't what you say or don't say. It's in your damned face—in your eyes—every time you look at me!'

Jed started to explain to her that it hadn't been that way—and realized in that instant how useless any words were now. He was aware of himself still breathing in the shallow, sucking way of a man completely exhausted. He glanced down at his hand holding the brim of his hat and saw that it was trembling slightly.

'Goodbye, Jenny.'

He strode from the kitchen.

★   ★   ★

Rose stood in the shadows by the window. From the street below came the sounds of roistering cowhands, the occasional clatter of hooves as someone spurred out of town. The sudden trill of a girl's laughter followed by the sound of a closing door echoed beneath their feet, deep within the bowels of Rose's Parlor House. Rose turned to face him.

'Then it's all over between you and Jenny, is it?'

'Yes,' Jed replied. He was sitting on the edge of Rose's big, canopied bed. 'And I figured you should be the first to know.'

'Why?'

'Because you were right. I was a fool.'

'Is that why you're here now? To tell me that you were a fool?' Her voice was barely audible. 'I already knew that.'

The light filtering in through the window caught the edges of her dark hair. In the dim light from the single lamp on her dresser, she looked quite young. Her figure, he knew, was still the envy of her girls. Her chin was full, her mouth generous, her lips together now in gentle fullness. Deep in their sockets, her dark, luminous eyes gleamed expectantly. He knew what she wanted him to say, but could not get himself to lie to her—even though he wanted to very much.

'No,' he said. 'That's not the only reason I came.'

'What's the other reason?'

'I scalded the back of my legs. The skin's already beginning to peel off.'

Her smile was swift. 'And *that's* the other reason?'

'You know how a burn can fester.'

'Yes,' she said emphatically. 'I do.' She moved quickly past him toward the door. 'Lay back on the bed and take off your pants. I'll go get Maisie.'

As she reached the door, Jed called her name softly. Her hand on the knob, she turned back to him.

'Thanks,' he said. 'You didn't need to let me in tonight. You don't owe me anything. Not after what I did.'

She pulled open the door, then paused in the doorway, looking back at him. 'Can you believe this, Jed? I was hoping it would work out for you and Jenny.'

'I can believe it, Rose.'

She pulled the door gently shut behind her.

★   ★   ★

Maisie was picking up the basin, the petroleum jelly, and the bandages, when Rose left his bedside, a sudden frown on her face, and went to the window. As the black servant girl hurried from the room, Jed glanced over at Rose. She was peering down at the dark street.

'What is it?' he asked.

'I heard something. Sounded like a shout. But it's too dark to make out what's going on down there. Wait a minute. Someone riding into town and there's a crowd following him.'

Jed grabbed his Levi's and stepped into them. As he was cursing his fly shut, he heard Rose's sudden intake of breath. He was beside her at the window in an instant.

The rider Rose had spoken of was just passing under a street lamp. Jed couldn't be positive, but it looked like one of the nesters—Sukeforth. He was leading a big black that had what looked like a body slung over the saddle. From the way it was carried—inside a sleeping bag—Jed had no doubt the body was already a corpse. As Jed watched, he saw Frank Corbett, his deputy, push through the crowd toward Sukeforth, who was pulling up in front of the jailhouse.

'Did you tell Frank you'd be up here?' Rose asked.

Jeff nodded.

'How do you feel? I mean the burn.'

73

'It feels a lot better. I should be able to ride now.'

'I hope you realize you're going to need more help than I can give you with Brewster's son on your trail.'

'Are you afraid of Brewster?'

'Everyone in Milk River County is afraid of Harlow Brewster.'

'There's no reason for Carl to be on my trail any more. He's got what he wants. And Jenny's something I don't want any more.'

'That's anger talking, Jed. And hurt.'

'But it's true. I guess a man should try at least once to turn a dream into something real. Then he should let it go and grow up, no matter how it hurts.'

'That's what Jenny was to you? A dream?'

'That's how it started, Rose. But you can't put a heart into a dream—or compassion, either. You reach out to hold it, and it's gone from you. It became a nightmare soon enough. Tonight was a surprise. Only it was a surprise I had expected. Anyway, it's over now.'

'You hope.'

"That's right. I hope.'

A sharp cry from the street drew their attention back to the crowd below them. It was quite noisy by this time. Jed could hear the shouting clearly now. Some of the cries were sharp, angry. As he watched, Jed saw his deputy dash out of the crowd, heading

74

toward Rose's Parlor House. When the man disappeared from sight under the window, Jed turned to Rose.

'I'll go down to meet Frank.'

He left Rose at the window and hurried to the door. Opening it, he glanced back at her.

'Come back soon, Jed,' she said. 'Don't stay away so long this time.'

Jed pulled the door shut and hurried down the stairs. Halfway down the second flight, he saw Frank below him, taking two steps at a time. Frank hauled up as he saw Jed moving swiftly down the stairs toward him.

'What's up?' Jed asked. 'What's Sukeforth doing in town at this hour?'

'You won't believe this, Jed. He just brought in Clayt Durant's body!'

'Durant? You sure?'

'That's what Sukeforth told me.'

The two men quickly descended the stairs and hurried out through the lobby into the night, heading for the crowd boiling around the jailhouse—and Clyde Sukeforth.

'Did Sukeforth kill Durant?' Jed asked, as Frank—a man smaller by at least a foot—hurried to keep up with Jed's ground-devouring stride.

'He says he didn't. Says he found Clayt's body in a line shack near North Fork Pass.'

Jed shook his head in disbelief. 'Sukeforth's a fool. Bringing in Clayt's body like this. Sundown don't like nesters, especially when they bring in a dead ranch foreman. No one is going to ask for particulars.'

'Except us,' Frank corrected him quickly.

'That's right. Except us.'

By that time they had reached the crowd. Jed went first, his broad, solid shoulders slicing a path through the noisy crush. When he gained the boardwalk, he saw Clyde Sukeforth cowering in the doorway of the jailhouse. The door was locked, so he had been unable to take refuge inside.

The crowd grew suddenly quiet as Jed pulled up in front of the nester. 'I understand you've brought in Clayt Durant's body.'

The nester bobbed his head quickly. 'He's over there on his horse. I found him. He was already dead when I found him, Sheriff. That's the truth!'

'I believe you, Sukeforth. Calm down.'

Jed turned to face the crowd. 'Go back to your bars or your homes, whichever. The excitement's over. Frank and I will handle this. Are you out there, Syd?'

Syd Mainwaring, the town's undertaker, raised a hand and began to push his way through the crowd toward Jed. 'Right here, Jed,' the fellow called. He was dressed as befits an undertaker, with the exception of the dust. His long, sharp nose was already purpling from the copious whiskey he downed to dull the smell of corpses and deaden the sound of weeping. Pulling up in front of Jed, he said wearily, 'You figure Harlow Brewster will pay for this one, Jed?'

'He should.'

As Syd led the black away through the thinning crowd, Frank opened the door to Jed's office. Sukeforth hurried inside, Jed right behind him.

'Sit down, Sukeforth.'

The man sat, gratefully, in a wooden chair by the desk. Watching him curiously, Frank sat down on Jed's bunk and leaned his back against the wall. The door to the cells was open, the cells all empty. Jed sat down in the swivel chair behind his desk and swung slowly to face the nester. The man had taken out a ratty polka-dotted handkerchief and was mopping his brow.

'I believe what you said out there, Sukeforth,' Jed told the man. 'But I am puzzled why you took such a chance— bringing in Clayt's body like this. In the middle of the night. You know how these people in Sundown feel about nesters. Their sympathies are with the cattlemen.'

'I know that, Sheriff. But I didn't see what else I could do. The man was dead. I found his body near our settlement. My son Will told me to bury the body and get rid of his horse. But that wouldn't have solved anything. His disappearance would have caused every rancher in the North Basin to go

77

against us. And I couldn't just leave him to rot. Like I didn't care. He should be buried decent, like any Christian.'

'Of course.'

'And besides, I trust you, Sheriff. You tried to stand up to Brewster today. Brewster's son had to club you to the ground to stop you. I judged you wrong before. And I'm here to say I'm sorry. And that I expect you to see to it that none of us settlers gets blamed for Clayt's death.'

'That's a tall order.'

'I know it. But, like I said. I trust you.'

'What can you tell me? I mean about finding Durant's body.'

'It was the shots that drew me to the line shack.'

'Shots?'

'Four of them. Will had said earlier he was sure riders from the Lazy 8 had followed us to the pass. When I heard the shots, I figured he was right, so I climbed up to the line shack where I thought the shots had come from. I saw Clayt's horse first, tethered in the pines. I got nervous and ducked in the line shack. And that was when I found Clayt's body.'

'He was dead?'

The man nodded gloomily. 'He was a mess, Sheriff—all tore to pieces, he was.'

'And that was the four shots you heard?'

'He had four wounds. It looked like whoever was firing, wasn't firing at us. And we didn't do it.' Sukeforth pulled a Colt from his belt. 'This gun was still warm when I found it beside his body, and it stank of gunpowder.'

'Did Clayt have a gun in his holster?'

'Nope. 'Pears to me this's his sidearm right here.'

Jed took the weapon from Sukeforth.

'Will and the others, they thought I was crazy to ride in here with Clayt's body, Sheriff. But you can see now, can't you. The truth will be my shield, and you just heard it.'

Jed smiled slightly at the nester. He believed the man. There was no guile in him; it was perhaps his touching, almost childlike trust that had gotten him into his present fix: a nester with little cash attempting to take range land away from the most powerful rancher in the county. And now, like an innocent child moving among lions, bringing in Clayt Durant's dead body in the middle of the night.

Of course, it wouldn't have made all that much difference if he had waited until daylight anyway.

'All right, Sukeforth,' Jed said, dropping the revolver into a top drawer. 'I know where I can reach you then—at the North Fork Pass.'

The man got to his feet, immensely relieved. 'I'll be there, Sheriff. I ain't goin' nowhere.'

The door burst open and Carl Brewster strode in. His lower jaw was swollen, and his eyes were smoky with rage. Two men were with him, his sidekicks from the Lazy 8. Phil Potter and Chuck Hammer. The two men were nasties, and Jed had it on good authority that Carl had hired these two gunslicks over his father's heated objections. They flanked Carl now with legs spread wide, arms folded.

Carl fixed his smoldering eyes on Jed. 'I heard this sonofabitch killed Clayt. That right, Sanford?'

'Don't look like it.'

Carl's face and neck reddened with fury. 'You covering for this damn nester again, Sheriff?'

'I didn't do so well this afternoon, Carl. But I plan to do better in the future. Sukeforth brought in Clayt's body. He said he didn't do it. And he has witnesses. I believe him.'

'Then, damn you! Who the hell *did* kill Clayt?'

'That's for me to find out.'

'He didn't have an enemy in the world! There's no one else, Sanford. No one else but this man standing here. Sure, he brought in Clayt's body. To make it look like he's innocent! You ain't gonna fall for that, are you? No matter how you feel about me!'

'It has nothing to do with how I feel about you, Carl. It has to do with law. There'll be

80

an inquest. You can testify at that inquest if you want to.'

Carl shook his head slowly. 'No, Sanford. I ain't going to testify at any inquest. There ain't gonna be one. This nester ain't gonna last that long.'

'I warn you, Carl. If you try...'

'Don't warn me, Sheriff. Just stop me. If you can.'

Then Carl turned and strode swiftly from the office. Jed got to his feet and followed out after the three men. There was still a thin crowd in front of the jailhouse; and as Carl and his two sidekicks mounted up, Carl gave an order to someone who was standing in the shadows across the street, something about keeping an eye out. Jed couldn't be sure, but he thought he caught the dull gleam of a shotgun in the man's arms.

Jed turned around and went back inside, closing the door securely behind him and bolting it. Then he looked at Sukeforth. The man had the appearance of one who has just been told someone close to him had died. His face had a bluish, papery cast to it.

'I think you'd better stay here for the night, Sukeforth,' Jed told him. 'It wouldn't be a good idea for you to ride back to your people tonight. You'll be safe here. Frank and I will see to that.'

'And tomorrow,' said Frank, 'things'll be calmed down. You wait and see.'

'That's right,' said Jed, doing his best to match his deputy's optimism.

'You mean I'll have to sleep in . . . there?' Sukeforth asked, slumping back into the chair.

'Sure,' said Frank, getting up from the cot and coming over to the nester. He placed a comforting hand on the man's shoulder. 'I'll be sleeping in the next cell, and Jed will be out here.' He smiled down at Sukeforth. 'I hope you don't snore.'

Sukeforth looked unhappily over at Jed. 'I . . . I guess I shouldn't have brought Clayt's body in. I should have listened to Will.'

'You did what you thought was right,' Jed replied, trying to comfort the man. 'Don't think no more about it. Go get some sleep. We'll escort you back to your people tomorrow morning.'

Sukeforth nodded and got slowly to his feet. Frank lit a lantern and went ahead of him through the door into the cell block. Jed went over to the wall rack, pulled down a Greener, split it, and began loading it. It was a ten gauge, and he was loading it with nine buck to the barrel.

CHAPTER SIX

Natalie awoke in a sick sweat, stretched naked across her bed. Her torn nightgown lay on the floor in a disordered heap. Peering through painful, slitted eyes at it, she vaguely remembered herself tearing the gown from her body when she tripped over its long skirt on her way across the room for the fresh bottle she had ordered Alice Lone Bear to bring to her. She had returned to the bed with the brandy. Naked, she had lain on her back and tipping the bottle high, had poured the poisonous brew down her throat, seeking oblivion.

She had achieved instead a fearful headache and a certainty that if she moved too abruptly, her head would tumble, broken, from her shoulders. She groaned as she tried to sit up. She was dimly aware that something had awakened her—something from outside the house. She held herself still and listened.

Dim shouts came from the compound. The sound of hooves, the jingle of bits. She could not understand it. It was black as pitch outside her two large windows. Moving slowly, she rolled over onto her stomach, pushed herself off the bed until her knees rested on the floor, then slowly stood up. Groaning softly to herself, she turned and

83

walked carefully to the window and looked down.

Lanterns had been lit and now hung from nails on the stable wall and alongside the door to the blacksmith's shop. In the garish, yellow light she saw that most of Lazy 8's home crew was mounted up and heading from the compound. She recognized her father and Carl leading them. Puzzled, she watched them ride into the night. She glanced skyward. A pale, gibbous moon hung over the world, like a walleye. She shuddered and turned away from the window. She had a numbing sense of events running out of control, slipping inexorably from her grasp.

She sat back down on the edge of her bed, aware of her small, glistening pendulous breasts, the sour, alcoholic stench that hung about her, the filthy taste in her mouth. And then a rebellion within her made itself known to her. Oh, my God, she thought. I'm going to get sick!

'Alice!' she cried, lurching to her feet and starting for the door. 'Alice!'

The door swung open a second or two later. Alice entered with surprising swiftness for a woman of her size, a large wooden tub in her hands . . .

Afterward, thoroughly chastened, Natalie lay on her bed, her back propped up with pillows, a blanket covering her nakedness. 'I feel so . . . so ugly,' she said.

84

Alice smiled and nodded her head slightly, concern mirrored in her dark, shining eyes. 'The whiskey not make you feel better?'

'Ugh! I've never taken that much at one time. I'll never be able to understand why men do it.' She shook her head wearily. 'It does no good, no good at all. I was sick at heart before. Now I am physically sick, as well.'

'You sleep now, you think?'

'Yes. If I can. Anything to get rid of this headache, this awful sick feeling in my stomach. I feel so clammy.'

'You will feel better in the morning. I will bring coffee. Much coffee.'

Natalie closed her eyes and leaned her head back. 'Yes, that might help.' She opened her eyes. Alice was turning to leave. 'Alice . . .? Where has father gone with all the men? That's what woke me in the first place. I saw Carl with him, as well. They rode off into the night.'

'They go to Sundown.'

'Sundown?' Natalie lifted her head from the pillow, a frown on her face.

The big woman had turned back around and now regarded Natalie impassively. Natalie knew at once that she knew something very important, but that Natalie would have to ask her before she told her anything. It was maddening at times, but this was the way Alice was. And she had been in their household now for nine years.

'Why on earth are they riding into Sundown at this hour?'

'To hang nester.'

Natalie forced herself to go slow. 'Which nester, Alice—and why would they want to hang him?'

'His name Sukeforth, I think. He killed Clayt Durant.'

Natalie leaned her head quickly against the pillow and closed her eyes. She thought she had felt sick before, but this was worse—far worse. If someone had come up suddenly and punched her brutally in the stomach, it would not feel as bad as she now felt. Oh, my God, she thought. Oh, my God. This can't be happening . . . !

Alice had moved closer and was peering intently down into her face when she opened her eyes again. 'You all right now?' Alice asked.

'No,' Natalie said, with some difficulty. 'No, I'm not all right.' She looked wildly past Alice. 'I must get dressed,' she said. 'Help me, Alice. I'll need my riding skirt and blouse. And send someone to get my horse ready!'

Alice stepped back from the bed, her face registering surprise for the first time in a very long time. 'You are sick! You fall off horse, I think.'

'*Do as I say!*'

The look of surprise on Alice's face disappeared on the instant. Without a sound, she turned her heavy body silently and moved swiftly toward Natalie's closet.

★　　★　　★

It was well past midnight and Sundown was reasonably quiet. Jed had managed to doze off for a couple of hours. But his restlessness would not let him sleep for longer than that. The shotgun in his hand, he stretched his shoulders back tightly and walked into the cell block to find both Frank and Sukeforth asleep in adjacent cells. The sound of their quiet snoring quieted the jumpiness that had fallen over him when first he sat up on his bunk and reached for the Greener. He turned from the cell block, walked across his office, and unlocked the door. Stepping out onto the porch, he sucked into his lungs the high, bracing air, and looked up at the moon. It was not quite full and shone with a kind of reddish glow. Its light did not comfort him.

Glancing across the street, he saw that Carl's man was still watching warily from the shadows of the general store, his own shotgun gleaming dully in his hands. The man was leaning back in a wooden chair, his back resting against the wall. The porch roof of the store enclosed him completely in shadows. Jed wished he knew who the man was.

It wouldn't be Potter or Chuck Hammer. Both men had ridden off with Carl.

Jed leaned back against the jailhouse wall, set his shotgun down beside him carefully, then took out some makings and built himself a smoke. When the match flared, he saw the watcher across the street right his chair and leaned forward alertly. He had probably been dozing.

As Jed sucked the smoke into his lungs, he felt himself quickening—and thinking once again of Carl Brewster and Jenny LaRue. It was quite possible, he realized, that Carl's business with Jenny had more to do with his hatred of Jed than any deep love he felt for Jenny. Ever since Jed had been made sheriff—as a result, primarily, of Harlow Brewster's powerful influence—Carl had waged a relentless campaign to turn Jed's allegiance to Harlow to his own advantage. But Jed had taken a fierce pride in the fact that he never gave an inch to the rancher's son, come hell or high water.

And now Carl had his revenge. There was not the slightest doubt in Jed's mind that this evening's discovery of Carl with Jenny had not been an accident. Carl had wanted Jed to find him with Jenny. Carl had taken his beating for it, but Carl had made his point. He had struck at Jed where he was most vulnerable. And he had used Jenny abominably to that end. In a way, Jed found

88

he could understand Carl's enmity. And perhaps Jenny's betrayal, as well. Some women detest pedestals, and he had tried to construct one for her, despite what they both knew she had been.

It was finished now between him and Jenny, Jed realized. But what he and Carl had going was not over. And this night, Jed was certain, would only deepen their enmity. He had no intention of allowing Carl to take Sukeforth, just as he had never had any intention of letting the man humiliate a clerk or threaten one of Rose's gamblers whenever Carl was in one of his drunken rages. Frequently, Rose was forced to call on Jed to assist Carl from her premises; and it was usually one of her girls who forced the issue. At these times, Jed found himself sickened by Carl's apparent behavior with these women. In his cups, the rancher's son revealed an appetite so depraved, so totally lacking in restraint, that it appalled even the most hardened of Rose's prostitutes.

Strangely enough, Harlow Brewster never objected to Jed's treatment of his son, no matter how often Jed flung Carl into a cell or booted him mercilessly out of a saloon and onto a horse—a fact that thoroughly infuriated Carl and was undoubtedly what had prompted Carl to send for his two gunslicks. Only recently had it dawned on Jed why Harlow had always backed

Jed—why, in fact, the man had done so much to help Jed become sheriff in the first place. Brewster had long since gained a whiff of the rot in Carl's soul, but, powerless to deal with it himself, he had gambled that Jed might be an authority who would stand up to Carl and perhaps straighten him out.

If that *had* been his intent, it had not worked. Not at all. Carl had simply grown more dangerous, and far more devious. And now, because of Sukeforth back there and the threat that he and his kind represented to Harlow Brewster, the rancher now found himself exploiting those very appetites of his son he had for so long tried to extinguish. In front of the Sukeforth cabin yesterday, Harlow Brewster had cut his son loose. The result had not been very pretty.

★   ★   ★

The dim thunder of hoofbeats broke into Jed's thoughts. He flicked his cigarette into the darkness, bent, and picked up the shotgun. The fellow in the shadows across the street got up from his chair and moved to the edge of the porch to peer down the street. Jed ducked quickly back into his office.

'Frank!' he called sharply.

He heard the squeak of a cot and the sound of hinges swinging back. Frank appeared in the cell block doorway, blinking the sleep out of his eyes.

'We got company,' Jed told him. 'Carl's back with his army, I'm pretty sure.'

Frank nodded briskly and stepped to the wall rack and pulled his Winchester. As he levered a fresh cartridge into its firing chamber, Sukeforth appeared in the doorway behind Frank. He looked scared.

'Will was right,' the man said, moistening his dry lips. 'I shouldn't have brought in Durant's body.'

'Now don't you worry,' said Frank, turning his blocky body to face the nester. 'They'll have to crawl over my dead body to get to you. Go on back inside that cell, and just let Jed and me handle this.'

'That's right,' said Jed. 'Be best if you stayed out of sight, Sukeforth. And let us do the talking.'

The man nodded shakily, turned, and vanished back into the cell block. Frank turned around and looked at Jed bleakly. The deputy was talking a whole hell of a lot braver than he was thinking. Jed turned and walked out onto the low porch to wait, Frank right beside him. As the first horsemen appeared out of the dimness at the far end of town, Frank pulled the door firmly shut behind them.

Brewster and his son were in the lead. Better than fifteen riders crowded close behind them as they clattered down the

91

street. As they came, townsmen who had been waiting for this moment stole from darkened stores and saloons and gathered in huddled clots or moved like furtive animals along the broadwalk, keeping up with the flow of the riders. Before the Lazy 8 contingent reached the jailhouse, however, Judge Eli Rawlins darted across the street toward Jed and Frank.

The little man was built like a small, weathered fence post, his forehead hidden perpetually by a flap of snow white hair. He was in his usual uniform: a black derby, dark broadcloth suit, battered boots. A black string tie was knotted at his neck. His shirt, as always was almost as white as his hair. Eli's square face was filled with concern.

'You can't let them do this, Jed,' he cried.

Jed grinned uneasily as the little man took his place beside him on the porch. 'I know that, Eli. And we sure as hell don't intend to.'

'I'm right beside you, boys.'

Frank smiled at him. 'We appreciate that, Judge.'

Brewster drew his horse up within a few feet of the jail, his horse swinging its lathered head unhappily, the cruel Spanish bit jingling loudly as it did so. Carl reined in beside him, and the thunder of the other horsemen gradually quieted as the rest of the Lazy 8's riders pulled up in a close semi-circle behind Brewster and his son. The crowd gathering behind the riders was surprisingly silent.

Through the crowd strode the fellow Carl had ordered to stay behind and keep an eye on the jailhouse. Jed recognized him as one of Carl's drinking buddies. To the right of Carl Jed saw Phil Potter and Chuck Hammer.

'He's still in there, Carl,' said the fellow with the shotgun, as he came to a halt beside Carl's horse.

'Figured he would be,' said Carl, dismounting.

At once Harlow, Potter, and Hammer dismounted also. As the five men started toward the jailhouse porch, Jed lifted his shotgun. 'Hold it right there, Harlow,' he said. 'Don't go any further. Sukeforth's in my custody—and that's where he's going to stay.'

Brewster hauled up. 'He killed Clayt!'

'If he did, he'll get a fair trial first—and then a hanging!' cried Judge Rawlins. 'You know better than to ride in here like this, inciting your men to lawlessness. And one of them your own son! This man standing beside me is a man you backed for office. You wanted law and order, and that's what you got! But it's not your law to change at will!'

Harlow Brewster's face had gone pale as the judge lit into him. 'That's some speech, Eli. But I ain't buying it. Not tonight, I ain't. The law you're talking about has let these damned squatters in, it's threatening to take my land, and now it's standing between me and the dirty nester that killed my foreman, my top hand! You think I can let that stand!'

'You'll just have to,' said Jed. 'Because I'll shoot the first one who sets a foot on this porch.'

'And I'll shoot the next one,' seconded Frank.

'If I had a gun,' quavered the judge angrily, 'I'd do the same thing!'

'Too bad you ain't got one, judge!' cried a horsemen behind Chuck Hammer.

As the rider spoke, he sent his rope in a wide loop out over Eli. The noose fell about the little man's shoulders, and before he could free himself, a vicious tug had tightened it snugly around his upper arms and yanked the startled judge off the porch.

With a cry, Frank reached out quickly and tried to pull the rope from around Eli. In so doing, he was pulled after the judge. Hammer's gun hand flew up. Jed saw the barrel of his six-gun gleaming in the moonlight and jumped off the porch to help Frank. He was too late as the barrel came down with brutal force on the deputy's head. Jed heard the sickening crunch as the top of Frank's skull broke under the force of the blow. Even Hammer seemed startled as he drew back and let Frank crumple in a heap at his feet.

By that time Jed was lunging for Hammer. He did not remember what he had done with his shotgun as he closed the fingers of both hands around Hammer's neck. He felt the vertebrae in Chuck's neck crunch and saw the man gasping as he fell back, eyes bulging. And then Jed heard as well as felt something extraordinarily heavy come crushing down on him. The last thing he felt as he sagged to the ground were his fingers loosening from around Hammer's neck.

★   ★   ★

Jed stirred and lifted his head off the damp ground. He could hear the dim roar of the crowd further down the street, near the livery stable. Jed pushed himself to his feet. He was finding it difficult to think clearly, but knew dimly that there was something urgent he must see to—and then he became aware of the odd heaviness at the back of his head. He blinked down at his hat on the ground, his shotgun beside it.

He reached up and touched his head. His fingers came away with blood on them. The touch had sent shards of pain plunging down into his skull. He turned carefully toward the sound of the crowd. As he did so, he saw the jail door hanging open—and lying in a heap in front of the low porch, the body of his deputy.

Oh, Christ! he thought, as he dropped beside Frank and rolled him over. The ominous heaviness of the body warned him, the man's wide, staring eyes confirmed it. Frank Corbett was a dead man, and in that instant the memory of what had happened swam back into Jed's befuddled consciousness. He saw again in his mind's eye Chuck Hammer's crushing blow to Frank's skull. He remembered also that as he lost consciousness, his fingers had released Hammer's neck. He glanced back again at the open jailhouse door. Sukeforth!

Jed reached over for his hat and placed it carefully onto his throbbing skull. Then he picked up his shotgun and started down the street at a steady, painful trot toward the crowd. Abruptly, a loud cheer rent the night. Jed slowed to a steady stride and swore bitterly. There was no doubt in his mind what that sudden cheering signified. Torches were smoking on the fringes of the mob, sending a livid, garish glow over the faces of the spectators. Every man was too intent on the sight of a fellow human being dancing on the end of a rope to notice Jed's steady progress through the moonlit night toward them.

The sound of a hard-galloping horse behind him caused Jed to turn. It was Natalie Brewster. She was wearing a black riding skirt and blouse. Her black sombrero had been swept off her head, its rawhide chin strap holding it in place. Bent forward over

96

the neck of her mount, she was furiously lashing its flanks with her quirt. The horse's chest and forelegs were ribboned with lather, its great eyes bulging out of its head. Natalie's face was bone-white and stark. She rode like she was the last survivor out of hell. Jed stepped quickly to one side as she swept past him toward the crowd.

It parted hastily for her. Jed heard her scream of horror and dismay. It sent a chill up his spine. He broke into a trot, despite the awful pounding in his skull, and drew up finally alongside Natalie's horse.

'Cut him down!' she was screaming at her father. 'You must cut him down!'

'Natalie!' her father pleaded. 'This is no place for you. What are you doing here? Get back to the ranch! This here's men's business. We've just hung the man who murdered Clayt!'

'Please!' Natalie cried, sobbing openly now. 'Oh, please! Cut him down!'

Jed looked past Harlow Brewster at the front of the livery stable. Harlow and Carl had remounted and were sitting their horses close by the hanging man. Sukeforth was not yet still. His long, pathetically thin body was twitching spasmodically, his head bent at a sharp angle, his face bluish, his tongue protruding grotesquely. As Jed watched, the body twisted slowly. Sukeforth appeared to be staring wildly, hopefully out over the crowd.

Jed snatched his six-gun from its holster and fired at the rope. He missed. His second round severed a strand. He fired a third time and the rope gave way. The body plunged heavily to the ground.

Brewster's horse and that of his son reared skittishly as the body landed between them. The other riders, stationed alongside the livery stable, had difficulty controlling their mounts as well. Jed saw that the man up in the livery's hayloft, the one who must have looped the rope over the hoist beam, was Phil Potter. Jed saw him draw his weapon. Jed fired up at the man and drove him back inside the loft.

Everyone around Jed fell back. Standing beside Carl Brewster's horse was Chuck Hammer. Holstering his six-gun, Jed brought up the shotgun as Hammer slapped leather and came up with his own weapon. But Jed's shotgun was quicker. Both barrels caught Hammer in the mid-section, tore him apart, and swept what was left of him back against the flanks of Harlow Brewster's horse. Both his horse and Natalie's began plunging in wild-eyed terror, as the members of the lynch mob abruptly dropped their torches, turned tail, and bolted for the darkness.

As Carl flung himself from his horse to kneel beside his fallen comrade, Judge Rawlins rushed up to Jed.

'Enough, Jed!' the man cried. 'Stop it! There's been too much killing already!'

Jed dropped the Greener. 'Sukeforth. Is he ... is he dead yet?'

A Lazy 8 rider, leading his horse, walked over to Sukeforth's body and looked down searchingly, then nudged the nester with his boot. 'Yeah,' the man said, looking over at Jed. 'He's dead.'

Jed looked up at Natalie then. Her horse was quiet now. She was holding the reins, her head bent, tears streaming down her face. The sound of her weeping filled the moonlit night. For Jed at that moment, it was the only sound in the world.

CHAPTER SEVEN

Natalie knew she could delay it no longer. Still, she was reluctant to push herself out of the deep, flowered armchair alongside her dresser where she had been sitting for most of the morning. She had bathed and was fully dressed, and had been for more than four hours. Alice Lone Bear had brought up her breakfast on a tray, but she had barely touched it. Yet she was not hungry.

Her father and Carl were downstairs, she knew, waiting for her. Twice Alice had appeared in her doorway to ask if she was ready to come down, that her father was waiting and wanted to speak with her. It had only caused Natalie to slump still deeper in the chair as she waved Alice out of her room. But it was almost noon, and there seemed no way she could postpone the confrontation any longer. She had long since decided what she must tell them and having made that decision helped. But not much.

With a deep sigh, she pushed herself out of the chair and left her room. On the stairs she paused. She had caught the deep, rumbling voice of her father and the tight, mean voice of her brother. The two were arguing bitterly, but softly. She started down again just as Alice Lone Bear appeared at the foot of the stairs. When Alice saw Natalie on the way down, her dark face revealed some relief and she turned quickly away and padded swiftly toward the kitchen. Almost at once the voices of her father and brother were stilled.

By the time she reached the foot of the stairs, both men were standing in the doorway that led from the kitchen to the dining room, waiting for her.

'Good morning, Natalie,' her father said, not unkindly.

'Morning, Pa,' Natalie replied, her voice sounding meek and small to her.

'Been waiting for you to come down.'

'I know, Pa.'

'Shall we go into the parlor?'

Natalie nodded and led the way through the dining room and into the parlor. She curled up on the leather sofa, pushing herself deep into one corner and tucking her legs under her. It gave her the sense of security—of solidity—she felt she needed if she were going to be able to withstand the storm that must soon break over her.

Carl sat in his favorite armchair alongside the huge fireplace, her father taking his position in front of it, his feet wide apart. His granitic face frightened her. She had always been able to stand up to him; and, since her mother's death, she had found herself in an almost privileged position as far as her father was concerned.

All that was gone now, she felt instinctively.

'Natalie,' the man growled, 'why in tarnation did you do that?'

'Do what?' she asked, knowing full well what her father was asking. She didn't know if it was hunger from lack of breakfast, but her stomach had suddenly become as tight as a knot.

'I mean that spectacle you made of yourself at the hanging of Sukeforth. That's what I mean. Hell, none of us likes a hanging. But it was only justice. That man had killed the best top hand this ranch is likely to see in a long, long time. Hell, I was priming that man to run this spread one day—if your brother found himself unable to withstand the temptations of Rose O'Toole's pleasure palace. Well now, Clayt's gone—and that little scrawny bastard had done it.'

'How can you be so sure?' she asked. She had the odd sense that this was not happening to her. That it was all a dream. In a moment she would wake up in her bed and the sun would be streaming in the window, and . . .

'How can I be sure? Why, woman, you told me yourself where Clayt had gone! Don't you remember? You said he was still scouting them homesteaders when you left him. Well, he didn't come back because he couldn't. Sukeforth must have seen him. Maybe the two had a shoot-out. I don't know the details and I don't care. He brought Clayt in and tried to hide behind Jed's skirts. But I've had enough with these squatters, and this should give them a fine idea of what's in store for them.'

Carl had stiffened earlier when his father mentioned Clayt's value to the ranch. Now he was on his feet, approaching the man. Alongside him, he said, 'Pa, I don't like that.'

Her father swung around to face his son. 'Don't like what!'

'What you said about Clayt—and me. That he was the best top hand we'd likely see in a while, and that you were thinking of letting him run this spread some day. Like I said before, I'm your son—your heir. This spread will be mine some day.'

'It's about time you realized that.'

'Well, I do.'

'I been noticing. You might be interested to know that I had just about given up on the idea of priming Clayt for the job. The men didn't like him all that well. And then you'd been showing signs of coming around. Not a damned bit too soon, I might add.'

But Carl was still angry. Natalie saw the fury in her brother's eyes—and the hurt. For too long her father had cut him out. And for the first time, it seemed, she realized how little warmth there was between the two of them.

'I didn't like Clayt either,' Natalie heard herself say.

Her father nodded briskly. 'I noticed that, too. But that ain't no reason to carry on like you did. He was a top hand and served the Lazy 8 loyally and well. Hanging his murderer was only justice.'

'No, it wasn't, Pa.'

'Well, maybe you don't think so, Natalie. But you're just about the only one in these parts—except the damned squatters themselves—that thinks the way you do. And I'm surprised, I don't mind telling you.'

'Surprised?' Natalie looked numbly up at her father, the knot in her stomach tightening painfully.

'Yes, surprised. I was proud of you at

103

Sukeforth's cabin. You didn't cluck any then. You handled yourself rather well, I thought. Damned if you didn't. Yessir, I was proud.'

'I tried, Pa, to hate them like you did. I been trying to hate them now for the longest time. And I thought I did hate them. I was just as angry as you were at them for squatting on our land. I was furious at Jed for the way he appeared to be taking their side.'

Her father rocked back on his heels, looking carefully down at his daughter. His eyes were shrewdly appraising her. 'And now?' he asked her. 'You no longer feel that way?'

'I can't.'

'Why not? They are still our enemy. If the courts give them a go-ahead, they'll overrun our range like lice on a redskin's dog. We'll be finished. The Lazy 8 will be gone, shriveled up and hog-tied by barbed wire.'

'I know that, Pa. But when I saw Sukeforth riding off with those two cows, and his son sitting beside him on the wagon seat, I just felt awful.'

'I know.' Her father's voice was suddenly, surprisingly soft. 'I saw your tears.'

Natalie bowed her head. She was aware that tears had broken through again and were now coursing down her cheeks. 'I got something to tell you, Pa.'

'What, Natalie?'

'It's about Sukeforth.'

The man sighed. 'Let's not talk about him any more, girl,' he said, his voice still soft. 'The man's dead. He's paid his price. He'll serve as a reminder to the rest of his crowd. It is a sad thing, I know. But there's no reason why you should concern yourself with it any longer. We've got to put his death—and Clayt's—behind us. So we can save the Lazy 8.'

'That's right, Sis,' said Carl. 'The three of us got to hang together now. You got to forget all about Sukeforth.'

'But I can't!'

'Damn it!' her father exploded, his patience gone. 'Why can't you?'

'He didn't kill Clayt, Pa,' she cried desperately up at him, her vision distorted by her tears. 'I *know* he didn't.'

'What in tarnation do you mean?'

'I killed him, Pa! I killed Clayt Durant!'

Her father stiffened. It looked as if he'd been struck by something. Incredulous, he leaned forward. 'Do you know what you're saying, Natalie?'

'Of course I do.'

'*You* killed him?'

'Yes!'

'My God, Natalie! Why?'

'He ... he tried to rape me.'

'Oh, Jesus,' said her father. Everything solid in the man appeared to soften. He almost stumbled to the sofa and sat down

105

beside Natalie, taking one of her hands in his. 'It's all right, girl. It's going to be all right. Just . . . tell me what happened.'

'We were in the line shack. He . . . went after me, and when I told him he was finished at the Lazy 8, he just didn't care any more then. So I . . . made believe I would do what he wanted, then took his gun out of his holster.'

'Good for you, Sis,' said Carl. He was standing over both of them, listening intently.

'But he fooled me and slapped the gun away and grabbed me. I broke away from him and grabbed up the gun. He . . . he was coming at me, and I . . .' She buried her face in her hands and began to sob.

'That's all right,' her father said, quickly bending forward and taking her in his arms. 'You don't have to tell me the rest of it. You shot him. As you should have.'

Through her sobs, she cried, 'He . . . just kept coming . . . and I kept shooting and shooting . . .'

'That's enough, Natalie,' her father said soothingly, stroking her head and holding her close. 'That's all you have to tell me. I understand. I understand perfectly.'

Natalie heard Alice Lone Bear padding up to the sofa. She opened her eyes and looked up at the Indian.

'Alice,' said her father, 'take Natalie up to her room. Bring her what she wants. But I

106

think all she wants now is rest.' He looked back at her. 'That right, Natalie?'

She nodded, grateful. 'It feels better now, Pa,' she told him. 'It was awful keeping it inside me. But if only I had told you when I got back here, Sukeforth—'

He placed his rough hand over her mouth. 'Don't say another word of that. It was not your fault. You did what you could to stop us. Now go on back upstairs and rest up. Everything is going to be all right.'

Natalie nodded obediently and got back onto her feet. She was grateful for Alice's presence as she left the room. She looked back just once before she reached the stairs. Her father and Carl were standing together in the doorway, watching her.

At least now, maybe, those two will start working together, she thought bleakly, as she turned back around and started up the stairs with Alice Lone Bear.

'Natalie!' It was her father calling to her.

She stopped and looked back down. Her father was at the foot of the stairs. 'Yes, Pa?'

'You are to tell no one of what you just told Carl and me. You understand?'

Natalie nodded, but the tone of her father's voice caused a grayness to fall over her, a renewal of the sense of guilt she had been feeling all morning. She must not tell anyone. She must hide her dirty little secret. She felt like a chastised child who had just been caught with her hand in the cookie jar—only this was so frighteningly worse.

'No one, Natalie,' repeated her brother, striding up to stand beside her father.

'All right,' she managed, her voice barely audible.

She felt Alice Lone Bear's hand on her arm and let the housekeeper gently urge her on up the stairs. It was not over, she realized. Telling it had not helped. For the rest of her life Natalie would have to hide from the world what she had done in that miserable little line shack.

And suddenly she was seeing, not Clayt coming for her in the dimness of that shack, but the horribly distended face of the nester Sukeforth as he twisted slowly about on the end of that rope...

She was crying bitterly as she entered her room.

⋆　　⋆　　⋆

Jed and Eli were sitting quietly in the corner of the Cattleman, sipping their beers slowly. Will Sukeforth and Zeke Summerworth had just left the saloon. They had entered without a fuss, said their piece, and left. Jed had heard them both out without protest, nodded solemnly when they finished, and was now thinking over their words as he sipped the cool beer.

Will was no longer the belligerent, ungovernable cub that Jed had had to slap into submission the last time they had met in this saloon. He had spoken reasonably, measuring his words carefully, and not once blustering or threatening the sheriff he blamed for his father's death.

What he had announced, however, was nothing short of a declaration of war.

'You think Will can get them other settlers to go along with him?' Eli asked finally, just before he finished his glass.

Jed nodded. 'I don't see why not. Unless I can find out who did kill Clayt and bring him in.'

'That won't bring back Sukeforth.'

'It'll clear his name for sure. Then I can swear out a warrant for the two men who were the ringleaders of that lynching.'

'Warrants for Brewster and his son?'

'That's what I said.'

Eli thought a moment, his square face intent. 'Well, I'll sure as hell swear out the warrants, if you'll serve them. And maybe—just maybe—that might settle them nesters down some.' He looked quizzically at Jed. 'Why do you suppose Will Sukeforth was that quiet, Jed? He sure didn't bluster as much as I thought he would.'

'Maybe he's growing up. And besides, Eli, he knew about Frank. I met him earlier at Mainwaring's parlor. He inquired about the other two coffins, so I explained about Chuck Hammer and Frank. It sobered him a mite.'

'Think he blames you for his Pa's death then?'

'I'm sure he does.' Jed tipped up his stein and finished the beer. 'And I don't blame him one bit.'

Syd Mainwaring and Doc Wynant entered the saloon, obviously looking for someone. Jed waved to them, and at once they headed for his table.

'Looking for someone?' Jed asked them.

'We found him,' said Doc Wynant.

Eli started to get up.

'Stay put, Judge,' said Mainwaring. 'I think you ought to hear this, too.'

The two men pulled up chairs and sat down at the table opposite each other. Mainwaring scratched at his long, sharp nose and looked expectantly back at the bar. He caught the barkeep's eye and beckoned him over, then looked across at the doctor.

'You open, Doc,' he said.

Doc Wynant was a frail, birdlike man. He wore wire spectacles and a dusty derby hat. He took it off now and revealed a shiny, bald pate. Pursing his thin lips, he leaned toward Jed, his sharp, blue eyes gleaming. 'What Sukeforth told you was right, Jed. Clayt had four bullet holes in him.'

'So?'

'But not all four bullets were fired from

110

Clayt's gun.'

Jed frowned. 'How the hell do you know that?'

The barkeep arrived then, took Mainwaring's and Wynant's order, and retreated back to the bar. When he was gone, the doctor answered.

'The slug that killed Clayt entered from his back. The bullet struck him in the spine, then ranged up through his lungs and came to rest in his right ventricle. It did a hell of a lot of damage and was undoubtedly the fatal round. The other three rounds did damage, but not one of them would have proven fatal if he could have stemmed the flow of blood. I am not saying the other three rounds wouldn't have killed him, but it would have taken a while. But what killed him—and instantly, I'd say—was the round he took in the back.'

'And you think that round came after the others.'

'Seems likely. Did Sukeforth say how he found Clayt's body? I mean, was Clayt on his back or on his stomach?'

'Sukeforth didn't say.'

'Do you think his son would know?'

'He might.'

'I suggest you ask him.'

'Why?'

'Because I'm curious, Jed. Like I said. All four bullets were not fired from Clayt's revolver. And the bullet that was fatal was the one that didn't come from his gun.'

'Go on, Doc.'

'The round that killed him—I dug it out because I was curious to see what could cause such extensive damage—was a .44/40, and must have come from a Winchester at close range. Clayt's six-gun was a Navy Colt .36.'

'You mean it was two men who cut down Clayt?'

'Could be.'

'And it could be,' broke in Eli, 'that whoever killed Clayt saw the man was still alive after he had emptied three shots into him from Clayt's gun, so he went to his Winchester to make sure.'

Mainwaring looked at Jed. 'Someone really wanted that poor sonofabitch dead.'

As the barkeep brought Mainwaring and Wynant's drinks, Jed considered the undertaker's remark. Then he said, 'The trouble is, that won't wash. When Carl said Clayt had no enemies, he was right. I don't know anyone who hated Clayt Durant that much. His men maybe didn't think he was the greatest ramrod in the world, but the feeling against him was not that bad. He paid his debts. And he was in solid with his boss, Harlow Brewster.'

'Hell,' said Mainwaring. 'A lot of people around here figured he was going to end up marrying the boss's daughter before long. No question how he felt about her.'

'And I don't figure, considering the rate at which Carl puts it away,' Doc Wynant said, 'that Brewster would have minded one bit. Clayt was a top hand. Married to Natalie, he'd be able to take up the slack as Brewster got older.'

'You know what you're saying, don't you,' said Eli.

'What're we sayin', Judge?' Wynant asked.

'That maybe one of them nesters killed Clayt. Hell, maybe it *was* Sukeforth killed him, after all.'

'No,' said Jed.

'What about that son of his, Will?' the judge asked.

Jed frowned and sat back in his chair. 'Maybe,' he said. 'But we don't know. And sitting here is not going to tell anything.' Wearily, Jed pushed himself to his feet.

'Where you off to?'

'North Fork Pass. Think it might be a good idea to check with Will Sukeforth. See what he can tell me. Then I'll take a look around that line shack. See what I can dig up.'

'That's a long ride,' said the doctor. 'How's that gash on the back of your head? You should be resting up some, by rights.'

'Don't have the time, Doc.'

Jed nodded his goodbyes to the three men and left the saloon. *Doc Wynant was right.* It

113

was a long ride, and maybe it would be all for nothing. But if he wanted to prevent Will Sukeforth and the rest of those nesters from starting a bloody range war, he had better find out who *did* kill Clayt Durant.

And soon.

CHAPTER EIGHT

A sullen Will Sukeforth walked ahead of Jed into the line shack and pointed to a spot on the dirt floor.

'Right there,' Will said. 'Pa didn't touch Clayt when he found him first time. He didn't need to. He saw the big hole in Clayt's back and the other wounds and realized Clayt had to be dead. Then he went down for Zeke and me. That was when we moved him, so we could dump him into his soogan and tied him to his horse.'

'And he was lying face down. Right here.'

'That's what I said.'

'Can you give me a rough idea of where his head was and his feet?'

Will thought a moment, then went outside. He returned a moment later with a sharp twig and swiftly drew an outline on the dirt floor. The head, the shoulders, and the torso were easily recognizable. Jed thanked Will and studied the outline carefully.

114

It looked as if whoever fired into Clayt's back could have done so through the open window on the far side of the door. Could have. The gunman could just as easily have entered the line shack after wounding Clayt with his own revolver, then shot him in the back with his own Winchester. Just to make damn sure, as Eli had suggested.

Jed looked at Will. 'There should be some casings on the floor. Help me find them.'

'Help yourself.'

'You want to clear your father?'

'Is that why you're here?'

'Why else?'

'I don't believe you. I heard your questions down there. You suspect one of us. Maybe you think Pa *did* shoot Clayt.'

'All I know is that *someone* did. I don't think your father shot Clayt. But I have to find out who did if I am going to be able to clear your father and go after Harlow Brewster and his son.'

Will looked at Jed for a long moment, his face cold, his eyes filled with pain and hostility. Jed could understand how the boy felt. He knew how he himself felt about Frank Corbett's death. The man had been a loyal deputy and a good friend. But Will had lost a father. Jed said nothing further to inflame the young man and waited.

The anger in Will's eyes faded and a sad weariness took its place. 'All right,' he said

115

resignedly. 'I'll help you look.'

The two men squinted down at the dirt floor. Not much light filtered in through the two windows and the door, but the casings were not too difficult to spot. Will found one of them, Jed the other two. Three casings. .36 caliber. And that was all.

At Jed's suggestion, they went outside and searched the ground near both windows. Close in under a window, gleaming in the sunlight, Jed spotted the .44/40 shell casing. He picked it up and glanced in the window. It was the one on the far side of the door.

'Four casings,' Jed told Will. 'Three inside, one outside. You see why I'm asking questions, Will?'

The young man folded his long, narrow fingers over his thin, lantern jaw and considered the three shells that Jed held out to him. Then he glanced at Jed. 'Two people shot Clayt. Is that what you think?'

'Be pretty funny, wouldn't it, for someone to shoot Clayt three times in the cabin, then go outside, grab his rifle and shoot him in the back through the window?'

'Funny, maybe, but not impossible.'

'Well, anyway, you can see why I'm nosing around. And why I'd be grateful for any help you and your friends could give me.'

'I'll tell you what help we'll give you, Sheriff. After my Pa's funeral, the rest of us are going to take after these North Basin

116

ranchers, one after the other. And we're going to start with the Lazy 8. There's maybe four families down there in the pass, but we've got friends and kinfolks all over this here country. They'll be here for the funeral. And they'll be here for what comes after.'

'That's foolish talk, Will.'

'It is no more foolish than cringing every time a man on horseback appears on a ridge. It is no more foolish than waiting for the courts to give us our rights. It is no more foolish than letting my father get lynched for bringing in a dead man, and it is no more foolish than having our homesteads burned to the ground while the law stands by and lets it happen.'

'I did what I could, Will.'

'And that's what we are going to do, Sheriff. It couldn't be much worse than your best effort. So go on back to your office. Forget about who killed Clayt Durant. Forget about trying to bring Harlow Brewster and his son before the bar of justice.' Will smiled coldly. 'There's another kind of justice that Harlow knows all about. The rope. Well, we can use a rope, too.'

'I'd still appreciate any help you could give me.' Jed said wearily.

Will shook his head. 'You don't give up easy, do you.'

'No,' Jed said, 'I don't.'

'I told you all I know, and so didn't

everyone down there tell you what they knew. We heard four shots. It spooked us. We were scared. I'd seen riders, Lazy 8 riders, on our trail earlier. Pa went up to investigate. He came back down soon enough and told us about Clayt's body. Zeke and I helped Pa tie the body to Clayt's horse. I tried to talk Pa out of riding into Sundown, but he had great confidence in you. He saw how you tried to stand up to Brewster. It didn't seem to make no difference to him that you weren't able to prevent us getting run off our land.'

'You say you saw riders.'

'That's right.'

'How many?'

'Two.'

'Were they close enough for you to see their faces? Could you recognize either of them?'

'They were too far away.'

'One of them could have been Clayt.'

'That's right.'

'And the other could have been his murderer.'

'I suppose.'

'How long after you saw the riders did the shooting take place?'

'An hour or two, I'd say.'

Jed frowned. That was too long a lapse for him to be sure of a connection. Those two riders could have been from any of the ranches in the North Basin. There was no reason why one of them had to be Clayt. Still, it was something...

'Thanks, Will,' Jed said, heading for his horse. 'Guess I'd better get back. It's getting late.'

'Got your evidence, Sheriff?' Will was mocking him.

Jed smiled slightly, vaulted into his saddle, and patted his coat pocket. 'I got the shells right in here, Will.'

Will reached up and held the horse's bridle. 'It's not that I don't trust you, Sheriff,' he said. 'I just think you're in too deep. Harlow Brewster is too big for you or anyone else to stop legally. I realize that now. I wish I had realized it earlier.'

'And what *will* stop Brewster?'

'Force. Naked, unbridled force.' Sukeforth's eyes glinted coldly, purposefully up at Jed. 'And bloodshed. Harlow Brewster has sown a wind. Now let him reap his whirlwind.'

'Doesn't that apply to both sides in this?'

'If it does, I don't care,' Will replied bleakly, letting go of Jed's horse and stepping back. 'I am willing to pay any price to bring that man and his evil brood to their knees. Any price.'

Jed pulled his horse around and rode off through the pines without glancing back at the skeletal figure peering after him. Harlow Brewster had created in Sukeforth's son an

119

implacable foe—a man fired by only one desire: to destroy utterly Harlow Brewster.

And of course it would not make the slightest difference to Will Sukeforth what happened to him in the course of his vendetta. He had already lost everything that really mattered to him.

★　　★　　★

During the rest of the afternoon, as Jed rode deeper into the North Basin on his way to the Lazy 8 ranch house, he went over in his mind once again his reasons for undertaking this ride. First of all, he wanted to inform Harlow Brewster just what his action in lynching Clyde Sukeforth meant, legally, Jed was eager to put the matter to Brewster quickly and without equivocation: Jed held him and his son guilty of inciting that mob. He was, therefore, guilty of murder. No jury of Brewster's peers would convict him of such a crime, of course. But that did not matter to Jed. He wanted Brewster to know what he thought—and also that he intended to bring the man and his son in for a trial, no matter what the verdict might be.

And then there was the matter of Natalie's behavior. Hearing her father's plan to lynch Sukeforth, she had ridden through the night like a madwoman in a desperate, but vain attempt to stop the lynching.

Earlier that same day Jed had seen her astride her horse, watching impassively the manhandling of Clyde Sukeforth, the wounding of his son, the destruction of his homestead. It had not surprised him—that apparent willingness to see the nesters punished for trespassing on North Basin land—since she had made perfectly clear to him earlier just how implacable was her determination to rid the Lazy 8 of their presence.

What, then, could have driven her to that remarkable display of emotion at Sukeforth's lynching? She had revealed a despair that was truly soul wrenching. Jed could still hear her piercing scream of horror and dismay, her sobbing, pleading voice begging her father to cut Sukeforth down...

He had felt it then—and felt it now as he rode closer to the Lazy 8. Natalie Brewster knew who killed Clayt Durant. And it wasn't Clyde Sukeforth.

★   ★   ★

It was a little before sundown when Jed rode through the gate into the Lazy 8 compound. A group of hands was clustered on the porch in front of the cookshack. As he rode toward the big house, the group of men turned to face him. They made no effort to approach or to welcome him. Jed continued on toward the

121

house and saw Natalie appear from around the corner.

He waved to her in greeting and nudged his horse in her direction. As he neared her, he saw the ragged look on her face, the washed-out eyes. She seemed limp, as if she had been washed and hung out to dry.

The slanting sunlight was in her eyes. She shaded them as she glanced up at him. 'Light and set, Jed,' she said wistfully. 'What brings you this far? Haven't you seen enough of the Brewsters?'

Dismounting, Jed said, 'Not yet.'

Natalie called over to the group of cowhands in front of cookshack, asking one of the men to see to Jed's horse. 'This is your horseflesh, Natalie,' he reminded her. 'Tell your man to saddle my own for me, will you?'

'Oh, yes,' she said. 'I forgot, Jed.'

As Jed watched her with the hand she had called over and listened to her instructing him, he was impressed with her apparent lack of emotion. She was drained completely, it seemed. The lynching, of course.

And something else—something darker, he was certain now.

Jed heard heavy footsteps on the big house's porch. Turning, he saw Harlow Brewster, his son at his heels, coming to a halt on the edge of the porch, his eyes hard as he looked questioningly at Jed.

'What do you want, Sheriff?'

'I'd like to talk to Natalie for a minute or so, then I'd appreciate the chance to speak to both you and Carl.'

'What do you want with Natalie?' Carl demanded.

'I just want to talk to her, is all.'

'That ain't good enough. You're not welcome here, Sheriff. There was no need for you to shoot Chuck Hammer like that.'

'I see. I should have let him gun me down, kill me like he did Frank. Is that it?'

Harlow turned on his son. 'Shut up, Carl.'

Carl's face reddened, but the young man swallowed his anger and held his tongue. Harlow looked back at Jed. 'Speak to Natalie if you want, Jed,' the big man said wearily. 'But I don't want you badgering her. She's ... been through enough.'

'I'm all right, Pa,' Natalie said, smiling bravely at her father. 'Jed's badge doesn't scare me.' She looked at Jed squarely then and tried to keep the smile in place. 'Does it, Jed?'

'Guess not, Natalie. Maybe we can go over to the corral?'

Without a word, Natalie walked over to the corral fence through the swiftly gathering darkness. When they reached the fence, she turned to face him and leaned back against the gate, crossing her arms, her head tipped slightly, her eyes narrow. She was on guard, Jed realized, waiting to parry his first thrust.

123

She saw him as an adversary, someone from whom she had to hide the truth.

'You seem tired, Natalie—bone tired.'

'Do you blame me? Clayt's death, the lynching ... all of it. The horror!'

'Well,' Jed persisted ruthlessly, 'if this is what it takes to rid the North Basin of those squatters ...' He shrugged.

Natalie straightened. 'Oh, damn you, Jed,' she said softly, her arms dropping to her side. 'That was a terrible mean thing to say.'

'Maybe.'

'You know it was!'

'Is that so?'

'Yes!'

'Natalie, you know who killed Clayt. Tell me who it was.'

Natalie reacted as if Jed had slapped her. She shrank back from him, her mouth dropping open in surprise. Her face had been flushed with anger a moment before; now it was a bloodless, deathly pale.

'Go ahead, Natalie. Tell me. Get it off your chest.'

'You must be crazy, Jed!'

But there was no conviction in her words. And her eyes darted from side to side in their sockets. She looked for all the world like a cornered rabbit searching for a direction in which to run.

'No,' he said, reasonably, gently almost. 'I'm not crazy. But I was at the lynching too, don't forget. I saw you. I can hear you weeping still. There was a reason you rode into town like that. It was in your scream. Your despair, Natalie. It is in you right now. The knowledge that Clyde Sukeforth did not kill Clayt Durant.'

'Oh, God, Jed!'

'It wasn't Sukeforth, was it?'

She shook her head, her eyes shutting tightly as she did so, tears squeezing out from under her eyelids and coursing untouched down her cheeks. 'No, Jed. It wasn't.'

'Then who did?'

'Please, Jed...'

'Tell me, Natalie!'

She opened her eyes and looked up into his face. He saw a scared, terrified little girl. '*I* did, Jed! *I* killed him!'

Jed was staggered. 'Now, wait a minute, Natalie! What are you trying to tell me, anyway?'

'You heard me! Clayt's death is on my hands, Jed!'

'But ... you and him. I mean, you and Clayt were going to...'

'That's what he thought, too,' she said with sudden bitterness. With the back of her hand she brushed angrily at her tears. 'But that was not what I wanted.'

At once Jed saw it all. 'You mean Clayt tried to—'

'Yes,' Natalie snapped. 'Pa sent Clayt and I

125

to keep an eye on the settlers at the pass. He was hoping they would all pull out when they got word of what happened to Sukeforth. Clayt and I were alone in the line shack, watching the settlers in the pass.' She looked bleakly up at Jed. 'He came at me, Jed. He was like an animal.'

'So you shot him. With his own gun.'

She nodded her head, then closed her eyes and turned completely around. With her back to him, her face leaning against the corral's fence post, she said, 'I won't testify in a court to that, Jed. I will deny I ever told you this. Do you understand? You can't make me get up onto a witness stand and describe what happened to me in that shack. It was too ugly. I won't go through it. Every time I think of it, I crawl all over. It makes me feel so ... so unclean.'

Jed took her gently by the shoulders and tried to turn her around to face him. She grew rigid under his fingers. He felt her entire body tensing in panic. 'Please, Jed!' she cried. 'Take your hands off me!'

'You heard her, Sheriff!'

Jed whirled to see Carl Brewster hurrying across the yard toward them.

'You all right, Sis?' Carl asked, hauling up alongside Jed.

Natalie turned to look at her brother. 'I told him, Carl.'

'Jesus, Natalie!'

126

Her face colored. In a hushed voice, she said, 'Don't curse at me! Don't you dare!'

Then suddenly, her head down, she bolted past them and ran toward the house. Jed thought he could hear her broken sobs as she ran. He turned to Carl.

'I'm not going to force Natalie to get up in a court of law, Carl. But maybe I'll want a statement from her. And right now I'm giving you and your father warning. I'm going to do what I can to make you regret that lynching. Both of you. The governor has already requested information, and I believe the attorney-general is interested as well. Some Eastern newspapers have carried the story, too.'

'That doesn't mean anything. They'll soon forget it. And who the hell do you think helped pay a good chunk of the governor's election bill last time?' He grinned at Jed.

'Well,' Jed said, bottling the anger he always felt when confronted with this insolent young Turk. 'You ain't finished with that business yet, no matter who you know. If the attorney-general doesn't sit on both of you pretty hard, you're still going to have the nesters to deal with.'

'What's that about the nesters?' It was Harlow Brewster, moving toward them out of the shadows of the big house.

Carl replied. 'The sheriff thinks the governor's gonna take after us now—and if that don't work, he's going to sic the nesters on us.' Carl couldn't keep the mirth he felt out of his voice.

'Get off this ranch, Jed,' Harlow said coldly. 'You just sent Natalie into the house crying after you wrung her story out of her. You had no call to do that. What did Natalie ever do to you? You've worn out your welcome at the Lazy 8, Sheriff. Get on your horse and ride out. Now.'

'Sorry you feel that way, Harlow. And tell Natalie I'm sorry if I upset her.'

'Just get out of here, Sheriff,' said Carl, a cruel smile on his face. 'Hurry on back to Sundown so you can check on your woman.'

Jed brought up the back of his right hand and caught Carl a stinging blow to his right cheek, then with his open palm caught him on the left side. The two cracks sounded sharply in the still evening air. Jed was sure the watching cowhands still in front of the cookshack heard them clearly. The force of the two slaps sent Carl back against his father. When he started to pull free of Harlow to come after Jed, Harlow held his son.

'You asked for that, Carl!' he snapped angrily. 'Now stay put.'

Jed touched the brim of his Stetson to Harlow and started for the barn—where his horse, the one Natalie had instructed the hand to saddle for him, was waiting.

* * *

After a silent, gloomy supper, which Alice
Lone Bear served as swiftly and as
unobstrusively as she could, Natalie declined
dessert and pushed her chair away, intent
only on getting back up to her room. It was
where she should have been—and
stayed—when Jed rode in.

But she was not to escape that easily.
Harlow and Carl pushed their chairs back
also, as if her move had been a signal to them.
At once she realized it had. They had been
waiting for her to finish.

'Natalie,' her father said. 'Let's go into the
parlor. We have to discuss this business with
Jed.'

'I'm tired, Pa,' Natalie protested. 'I don't
want to talk about it anymore!'

'I can understand that. But we're going to
have to talk about it sometime, and now, is as
good a time as any.'

'We don't have any choice, Natalie,'
chimed in Carl, leaning across the table
toward her, his voice urgent. 'Jed's not going
to leave you alone now!'

'I told him I wouldn't testify. And I won't!
I won't admit to what I told him!'

'He told me he's coming back to get a
written statement from you!'

'I . . . I won't give it to him!'

'Into the parlor,' said her father, turning

abruptly and stalking from the dining room ahead of them. 'We're going to discuss this calmly!'

With sinking heart, Natalie followed her father and Carl into the parlor and curled herself up on the couch, inwardly bracing herself as she awaited the onslaught.

A grim frown on his face, his feet planted solidly on the floor, and his hands tucked behind his back, her father faced Natalie. 'You shouldn't have told Jed anything,' he told her.

'That's right, Sis,' chimed in Carl.

'I know that, Pa,' Natalie replied, doing her best to ignore her brother. 'But it was like he knew . . . all along.'

'How could he have known?'

'It was the way I acted—when you lynched that man. He could see how I felt. Pa, I *had* to tell him. When he looked at me the way he did, and the things he said . . .' She shook her head and looked away from her father, determined that she was not going to cry this time, but aware of the ache in her throat, of the growing revolt within her, the pressing *need* to cry.

'All right, Natalie. It's done. We don't need to go over that,' her father said, his voice no longer accusing her. 'But what will you do if he comes here for a statement from you?'

'You mean I won't have to go on a stand in

front of everybody, just write it down?'

'Something like that, I guess. Yes. Would you do it?'

'I don't know. I don't *want* to. But if I have to, if he *makes* me ...!' The tears broke through and she felt them streaming down her face. 'Pa, what am I going to do?'

Carl stepped forward then. 'It ain't what you're going to do, Sis. It's what *we're* going to do that counts.'

Her father turned to face Carl. 'And just what are you suggesting, Carl?'

'Now, don't get on your high horse with me, Pa. It's time now for you to start treating me like I wasn't your second-hand son. You ain't got Clayt no more to lean on.'

'I remember,' said her father, his face hardening. 'You reminded me of this earlier, didn't you. You are my son and heir. Well, Carl, if you hadn't been so reluctant to *act* like my son, if you hadn't seemed so unwilling to pull your weight around here—you wouldn't have had to remind me.'

'All right,' Carl snapped. 'I'm pulling my weight now. Or haven't you noticed?'

'We won't argue the point, Carl. It is not something I want to argue with you about. Now, cut all this palaver and come to the point. What are we going to do about Jed? I'm listening.'

Still curled up on the couch watching the two men, Natalie shivered. There was something frightening growing between the two of them. She didn't know what it was, but it unsettled her, caused her to shudder inwardly. And then she had the sudden picture in her mind of her father and Carl as they sat their horses under the slowly twisting figure of Clyde Sukeforth.

'I'm going upstairs, Pa,' she cried, uncoiling from the sofa and hurrying from the room. 'I don't want to hear any more of this.'

Her father looked after her, concerned and puzzled by her abrupt departure. 'What is it, Natalie? What's wrong?'

She paused in the doorway and turned to look back at her father. 'Don't stop me, Pa. I am going up to my room, that's all.'

'But why are you rushing off now? We have things to discuss.'

'Then discuss them! With each other, but not with me I don't want to stay down here with you and Carl.'

'But ... why not?'

She took a deep breath. 'Because you *frighten* me! Both of you!' She turned swiftly and ran for the stairs.

Harlow Brewster made no attempt to go after his daughter. He heard her frantic feet on the stairs, waited for her door to slam, then turned back to Carl. Natalie's words troubled him. In an oddly unnerving way, she had made him fearful as well. Without a comment to his son, he went over to his

132

favorite armchair and slumped into it.

Carl remained standing. He walked over to the fireplace and reached down a hunting knife that had been left on the mantle. As he drew the blade along his forefinger to test its keenness, he glanced over at his father.

'You figure she's cracking?'

'I hope not. Natalie's a strong young woman. Perhaps even stronger than your mother. Stronger than you, maybe.'

'Sure. She was always your favorite. She could do no wrong, could she? Only now, it turns out, she's just killed Clayt Durant.'

'Stop that! You know damn well what happened.'

Carl looked at his father shrewdly. Harlow could tell that his boy was sizing him up and that he had just about finished testing the waters. An odd thought came to him: he didn't like his son.

'Yes,' said Carl. 'I know what happened. And now Jed knows. So we've got a problem, and here's how we're going to solve it.'

'I'm listening.'

'The newspapers will forget the lynching soon enough. And if what Jed said about them nesters is true, that don't worry me none. We can handle them. Every rancher in the North Basin is behind us. That leaves our sheriff, the man you wanted to see wearing that badge. He's the one we've got to worry about, not the governor or the

133

attorney-general. Him and his warrants and demands for sworn statements.'

'Get to the point, Carl.'

'The point is how to stop Jed. Not if we should, but how we do it.'

Harlow felt ice moving up his backbone. 'What are you proposing, Carl?'

'To kill the sonofabitch!' Carl smiled.

Harlow felt the cold reaching into his soul. This was his son talking. This was his son smiling as he proposes to murder a man. 'No,' Harlow managed. He shook his head. 'There's been enough—more than enough—killing. Don't speak of this to me again, ever.'

Carl frowned, his face darkening angrily. He peered closely down at his father. 'What's the matter, Pa? Did I shock you? Is that it?'

'Yes! You shocked me.'

'Hell, Pa, you knew all along what I was going to suggest. You weren't surprised one bit.'

Carl's words startled him. They startled him because he was not sure his son was wrong. Jed's death *would* solve much. Another sheriff was definitely needed. Jed had long since outgrown his usefulness. And yet, to hear his son suggest Jed's murder so casually had shocked him into an awareness of the horror of what he was contemplating deep inside. Now, as he looked up at his son, he had the feeling that Carl had some awesome power—that those insolent eyes of

134

his could bore into the very core of his soul.

'Maybe I wasn't surprised, Carl. Maybe I did think of it, at that. But now that we have considered it, I say forget it. We can't kill Jed.'

'No. I won't forget it. He'll destroy the Lazy 8. This is as much my ranch as yours, Pa. If you won't do what has to be done to save it, then I will.'

'It's not for you to tell me how to save this ranch!'

'It is if you won't!'

'I want no more killings!'

'Why?'

'Damn you, Carl. You know why. There's already been too many killings—more than enough for all of us!'

'Perhaps for you, old man. But not for me. And not for you, either.'

'Damn it! Make sense, Carl. What the hell do you mean by that?'

'Remember those four nesters back in Texas? You killed them easy enough. The nester and his woman—and their two boys. I saw it all, Pa. I was helping them fix that roof all that day. And you killed them. Then you turned around and rode back to the ranch. You thought I didn't know how you got that wound—the one that still makes you limp. And I guess you thought I'd never know why you finally had to move out of Texas.'

'My God, you *knew*!' Harlow whispered

hoarsely. 'Does ... does Natalie know as well?'

'I never told her.' He smiled icily. 'It was my secret. And now it's ours. So don't tell me we can't kill Jed Sanford. I know how a Brewster does what he has to when it comes to saving what's his.'

Harlow felt himself rising angrily from his chair. His hand in the air, about to slap sharply at his insolent son's face when he caught himself. He dropped his arm to his side and stared incredulously at Carl, a bleak, chill wind blowing through him. He felt suddenly older, much older. Until this moment he had never known his son.

'You're wrong, Carl,' he managed, slumping limply back into his chair. 'What happened in Texas was a mistake. That nester, he pulled a shotgun. It was all confusion after that, and when it was over, they were all dead. And two of my men, as well. I had not intended to kill any of them. Things just got out of hand.'

'Well, things are out of hand now, wouldn't you say? Do you want Natalie to testify—however she does it—to her having killed Clayt? Will anyone forget the lynching then? Are you ready to pull up stakes a second time, and move north? Is that what you want?'

'No. Of course not. But to murder Jed Sanford, coldly, deliberately...'

136

'Leave it to me, Pa. I know what has to be done—just like you did back in Texas. You might say I'm a chip off the old block.' He laughed softly, enjoying the effect that thrust had on his father.

'Get out, please,' said Harlow, looking up at his son.

'I'm going to town,' Carl said, turning swiftly and starting from the room. 'I think maybe I'll pay a visit to Jed's girl.'

Carl was chuckling at the thought as he disappeared.

For a long while Harlow Brewster sat without moving. All these years he had lived with this stranger who called himself his son. And during those years he had puzzled over and pondered interminably why his son had always defiantly gone his own way—willfully, without consideration for others, refusing to heed his father's counsel of moderation. He was like an errant, destructive force, a despair to his mother, a galling impediment to his father, a cruel, vicious tormentor of his sister.

The reason for Carl's behavior was now clear.

Harlow thought he had left behind him in Texas the awful legacy of that terrible night. Instead, he had brought it with him to this place in the person of his son. Over the years that scene of wild gunplay, with its violent, fatal consequences had grown like a cancer in his son's soul, turning him into something dead and unfeeling...

With tears streaming down his seamed cheeks, Harlow Brewster found himself recalling Carl's twelfth birthday when he had presented to Carl his present, a paint the boy had been admiring for months. It was a bright morning. Carl's shout of pleasure when Harlow had led the pony from the barn was still ringing in the air as Carl leaped into his father's arms.

Sitting now alone in his chair, Harlow Brewster thought he could still feel the strength in his boy's tough little arms as they squeezed happily about him. He had thought the boy was going to kiss him, but straightening swiftly, in a voice husky enough to mask the strong emotion he felt himself, he told the boy to mount up. Thrusting the pony's reins into his son's hands, he boosted him into the saddle.

Carl would have stayed on that pony all day if they had let him, and of course that night he pleaded with both his parents to be allowed to sleep in the barn with the pony. They had talked him out of it, but he was a very happy boy when he went to bed, and for the rest of that spring and early summer, Carl had ranged far and wide aboard the paint. The two were almost inseparable. And young Carl had grown much closer to his father as a result. The two often rode out together, each one proud to be seen with the other. Father and son inspecting what would soon be their domain.

They did not ride out together that fatal night, however, though both of them, it seemed, *had* ridden out...

Afterward, puzzled and hurt, Harlow Brewster had tried without success to recapture the easy camaraderie of that spring and summer. But for a reason he could not grasp, it had eluded him. His son had become distant, preoccupied. He seemed to be busy, always busy, elsewhere. For a while, after moving from Texas, Harlow had hoped the two would ride once again together over their lands as they had that distant summer before. But of course they hadn't. And they never would. Now at last Harlow Brewster knew why—and when—he had lost his son.

Long after the old rancher heard the hooves of his son's horse fading in the direction of Sundown, he wiped the tears from his face with his big, rough hands and got slowly, almost painfully to his feet. As he moved across the room, his limp seemed to have grown considerably more pronounced.

CHAPTER NINE

Troubled, Jed gazed down at the North Fork Pass settlement. It was growing. When last he had ridden out to inspect the line shack two days ago, there had been at most only four families making do in their shacks and tents along the stream. Now there were what appeared to be five more families settling in, one of them apparently living in their wagon. And if he was not mistaken, even at that moment another family was moving in a ragged line of wagons and livestock through the pass toward the settlement below him.

That would make ten families.

Jed urged his horse on down the slope. As it picked its way along the narrow game trail, he relaxed and gave the animal its head, his eyes still on the bustling settlement below him. Will Sukeforth and that long-bearded preacher seemed quite active, hurrying from one encampment to another, always drawing a crowd and seemingly doing all the talking. By the time Jed reached the floor of the pass, it looked as if Will had sent a mounted detachment to greet the new arrivals.

Will and the others awaited Jed as he neared the settlement. Long-legged young 'uns with flaxen hair and faces burnished from the sun had brought the news of his coming the moment he broke from the timber and started along the creek.

Will did not ask Jed to dismount as he pulled up in front of them. Besides Will and the preacher, there were at least eight other able-bodied men, all of them heavily armed, and each one of them, like Will and the preacher, with eyes hard and unyielding as they gazed up at him. They not only did not trust Jed, they did not like him.

'I'd like to dismount,' Jed said patiently, 'and coffee, if you have some.'

Not a single face softened. Jed looked at Will. The young man stared back at him with undisguised triumph in his eyes. Since that altercation in the Cattleman, Jed had no doubt, Will had been praying for this kind of a turnaround.

'Stay on your horse, Sheriff. I told you to go back to your office and forget about Clayt Durant, or who killed him. It don't matter no more. And we told you all we know.'

'Maybe,' said the preacher, taking a step closer to Jed, 'he's come here to accuse one of us of killing Clayt Durant.' The man smiled, his yellowing beard wrinkling grotesquely around his mouth. 'Maybe he thinks he can come by like this and pick us up one by one for Durant's murder. First your Pa, Will, then you, or me, then—'

'Shut up, old man,' said Jed, his voice cracking at the preacher like a whip.

Tanner pulled up, furious. He looked back at Will, expecting the boy to back him. Instead, Will stepped alongside the preacher, his face softening slightly.

'The preacher's a mite suspicious, Sheriff. Like all of us. We told you what we know.

141

There's no reason now for you to come by here, unless you're spying on us.'

'I think I might know who killed Durant,' Jed said. 'But the information I got doesn't quite fit together. I'd still like to clear your father's name, Will. Or aren't you interested in that?'

'The one you think did it,' Will asked, eyes narrowed cautiously, 'he ain't one of us?'

'No, not one of you.'

Will shrugged and turned his back on Jed. 'Light then. There's coffee at my fire.'

Tanner didn't like it, but he and the others dispersed after Jed took the coffee Will's mother handed to him a moment later around the fire. A narrow-faced, unhappy little girl of eight or nine clung to her weary mother and disappeared with the older woman when Jed sat down on a log before the low fire and gratefully sipped his coffee.

Will, watching him warily, sat on another log across the fire. He still held the Winchester he had been carrying when Jed rode in; now its barrel was leaning back against his right shoulder, its stock resting in the grass by Will's left foot.

'You don't like me much, do you, Will,' Jed said quietly, sipping the hot coffee. Will's mother had put honey in it, and its too-sweet taste bothered him.

'I won't soon forget how you treated me and Pa in the Cattleman,' Will admitted. 'But

I reckon you've been doin' what you can. Trouble is, your best ain't half good enough.'

'Yes,' Jed said wearily. 'That's the trouble, all right.'

'What do you want from me?'

'I want you to think back, real careful. Could those riders you said you saw following you, could either one of them have been Natalie Brewster?'

'Harlow Brewster's daughter?'

Jed nodded.

'Well, now. Like I said, they was too far away for me to see their faces.'

'Natalie was wearing a bright red blouse under her vest that day. I remember that clearly, and it seems to me something like that might stand out some distance.'

'Zeke Summerworth didn't ride back with us in the wagon,' Will said thoughtfully. 'He rode back on his horse. He said he saw the two horsemen, too. He might have noticed something.'

'Could I speak to him?'

Will got to his feet and called to one of the tow-headed urchins racing between the wagons. The kid responded instantly as soon as Will told him who he wanted. Will turned back to Jed then and sat down on the log. 'You want to tell me what this here line of questioning is leading to?'

'I'd rather not.'

'Suit yourself. Zeke will be here soon.'

143

Glancing past Will while he waited for Summerworth, Jed watched as the new arrivals were greeted by the others. Their wagon was a battered Conestoga and the interior seemed alive with kids. Walking alongside the wagon, however, were four husky, well-armed adult males, their faces hidden in thick, black beards. The rifles they carried gleamed in the afternoon sun.

'What are you doing here, Will?' Jed asked. 'Gathering an army together.'

Will smiled grimly. 'That's just what we're doing.'

'It won't settle anything, Will. Just cause more bloodshed. Wait for the courts to decide.'

Will laughed scornfully. 'The law!' he barked. 'I told you before I buried my father what I thought of the law. The rope is the law. For Harlow Brewster and now for us, too. Only I've changed my plans some. First we'll strip away Brewster's support. I figure once the other ranchers get a taste of what we've been eating for the past years, they'll maybe look the other way when we go after Brewster.'

'When is all this going to take place?'

'When we're ready.' Will indicated the family just settling in with a nod of his head. 'They came all the way from Kansas,' he said. 'We got more family comin' from Nebraska.'

At that moment, Zeke Summerworth

144

broke through the crush of wagons and tents and approached the fire. He looked at Will questioningly as he hauled up beside him. 'Benjy said you wanted me.'

Will nodded at Jed. 'He does.'

Zeke turned to look at Jed. 'What the hell do you want, Sheriff? You think maybe I might've killed that sonofabitch, Durant? Wish I had.'

'Did you see the two riders Will said he saw, the ones following you to this pass?'

'Yeah. I saw them.'

'Could you make out their faces?'

'Not too clear. But I didn't need to.'

'What do you mean?'

'I mean one of them was wearing a bright red shirt, a black sombrero and skirt. That figured to be Natalie Brewster. I got a close enough look at her when she and old Brewster were rousting us at the creek.' Zeke glanced at Will. 'You remember her, Will.'

'I remember,' Will replied, looking with sudden interest at Jed.

'Who do you think was riding with her, Zeke?'

'From the way he rode, her foreman Durant.'

'So you knew it was Clayt Durant and Natalie following you and the rest of the party from the creek.'

'Sure. I knew it.'

'But you didn't mention it to anyone?'

145

'I didn't think anything of it until Clyde found Clayt's body up there in the line shack. It was clear they was up there to keep an eye on us. The girl must have gone on back by herself, and that was probably when Durant got bushwhacked.'

Jed didn't say anything. He just looked at Zeke for a long moment. Slowly, Zeke's round face reddened and his eyes grew larger. 'Hey! You don't think Natalie killed Clayt, do you? The way I heard it, she and Durant were going to get hitched pretty damn soon, so Durant could take over the Lazy 8. That kid of Brewster's isn't worth a fart in a windstorm running a ranch, and his pa knew it.'

'I'm just asking questions,' Jed said quietly. 'I want to get to the bottom of Clayt's murder—to prove, if I can, that Will's father didn't kill him. Now, you say Natalie might have ridden back to the ranch alone. Did you see her ride out?'

'No. I didn't. Soon's I got here to the pass I was too busy to even think of it—until I heard them four shots coming from the line shack.'

'Thanks, Zeke. I might need your testimony later. If, that is, you and Will haven't turned this countryside into a battleground.'

'What the hell do you think it is right now?' Zeke demanded, as he turned and walked back to the wagons.

146

As soon as Zeke was out of earshot, Will said, 'It's Natalie Brewster then. That's who you think it is.'

'I'm not sure. It fits. But ... there's something else that bothers me about this, and you should remember it too.'

'What?'

'That fourth shot. Doc Wynant says it was the fatal one and that it struck Durant in the back. From the way you say Durant was lying when you and your father walked in, that means the shot came from the window, most likely. Outside. And you were with me when we found the casing.'

'Outside. At the window.'

'Yes.'

'I remember. Two people shot Durant, you think.'

'Yes.'

'But one of them was Natalie.'

'Maybe.'

'You *know* it was her.'

Jed didn't reply.

'And now you want the other one. Her accomplice.'

'It was the other one who fired the fatal wound, Will. There's a good chance Natalie's shots would not have proven fatal.'

'So ask her. Ask her who helped her kill Clayt Durant.'

'She doesn't know.'

'You asked her?'

147

'I didn't have to. I know she doesn't know. She thinks she is the one who killed Clayt Durant.'

'Well, then!'

'But she didn't. The thing is, someone finished Clayt Durant off and is letting Natalie think she's the one who killed him—all by herself.'

'It sounds crazy, Sheriff. Bring her in. See what she can tell you.' Then he smiled, wickedly. 'Only you can't bring her in, can you. She's a Brewster. Ain't a court in the world goin' to make Harlow Brewster's daughter fess up.'

'I am going to get a statement from her.'

'I'll believe that when I see it.'

'If I do, will you hold back on any crazy plans you and your people may have? Will you at least give me a chance?'

'It's gone too far, Sheriff. My Pa's dead. Our home's been burned to the ground. And Harlow Brewster and his crowd are still ridin' high, mighty high. You ain't going to get no statement from that girl. You'll get your ass shot off if you try, and you know that.'

'Maybe I will. At least give me a chance to try. If—like you say—I get my ass shot off, then it'll be your turn.'

Will looked at Jed for a long moment. 'All right, Sheriff. I got time still. Like I said, we got people ain't showed yet. Get your ass shot off by Brewster if you want. I'll hold back as

148

long as I can. Be interesting to see you walk into a buzz saw, the same one we been headin' into for the past year.'

Jed put his tin cup down on the ground beside the log and stood up. 'All right, Will. I'll do that. You know, I was at the funeral of your Pa. But you and your clan didn't show up for the funeral of a man who gave his life in an effort to save your Pa's life.'

Will frowned slightly and looked away from Jed's accusing eyes. 'You mean your deputy.'

'Yes. Frank Corbett. He was my deputy and a good friend. So you see, I have almost as good a reason to hate the Brewsters as you have. There's no reason you and I have to be on opposite sides in this. I'm doing what I can to help.'

'I know that, Sheriff,' Will said, looking contemptuously at him. 'But like I said before, your best just ain't half good enough.'

*   *   *

Jenny LaRue stirred sleepily, the heavy, droning voices boring into her sleep, pulling her into reluctant wakefulness. She opened her eyes and was able to see from her dark bedroom into the lighted kitchen. Carl was sitting at the table, his back to her, and the person he was talking to was not visible to her, but she could tell he was sitting at the

149

table across from Carl. She vaguely recalled the other person's voice; it might be Phil Potter, but not until she heard Carl address him as Phil during one urgent exchange was she positive that this was who it was.

Jenny turned her face away and buried her head in the pillow. She was exhausted; Carl and she had been going at it pretty hot and heavy earlier. His fierce, demanding insistence that she share his insatiable needs had drained her completely.

She closed her eyes tightly and tried not to let Carl's sharp, daggerlike thrusts of words and phrases keep her awake.

And then she heard Jed Sanford's name.

Instantly, the sense of loss she had been fighting these past few days overwhelmed her once again. Her anger at Jed's behavior was gone now, and in its place was a deep, agonizing sadness. A terrible perversity in her nature had made her hurt Jed, and allowed Carl to use her to get back at him. She had no illusions about it. Jed was lost to her forever now; the unlikely circumstance of a man treating her with respect and deep love, founded on mutual trust and respect, was one she would not soon find repeated. Certainly not from a man like Carl.

She blinked away the tears and rolled onto her back, alert. It was the quality of their conspiratorial laughter that alerted her to what they were planning. She held herself perfectly still and let the words sink in . . .

What they planned was complicated . . . and deadly. It just might work, she realized, a congealing dread growing in her heart. Carl would call Jed out. It would follow an argument in the Cattleman. Carl would appear in the street, waiting for Jed. When Jed showed, Carl would fire at him, then dart into the alley alongside the hotel. Once Jed entered the alley, he would be in Potter's line of fire. Potter would be waiting on the balcony over the hotel entrance. That would put Jed in a murderous crossfire. If Carl didn't get him from the front, Potter would from the back. And Potter would be firing a shotgun . . .

Jenny thrust a knuckle into her mouth to prevent herself from crying out in rage at the two men. With her teeth sinking into the skin of her knuckles, she heard Carl and Potter going over the details just once more. When he had finished, Jenny heard Potter voice his concern that Carl might not be able to call Jed out successfully, that he would be unable to anger Jed enough to make him follow Carl from the saloon. Carl laughed off that possibility. He reminded Potter of how furious Jed already was about him taking Jed's place between Jenny's legs.

Jenny writhed inwardly, shame washing over her. She closed her eyes tightly and did her best to hold in the rage that threatened to turn her into a fury. So intent was she on controlling her anger, she did not hear Carl's chair scraping against the floor as he got up. Only when she became aware of his shadow falling over did she realize he was in the doorway, staring in at her. Eyes wide, she turned her head to face him.

'How long you been awake, Jenny?'

'Not long ... I just woke up now. What's the matter?'

'Nothing.'

Carl turned and went back into the kitchen, out of sight. Jenny sat up on the bed, her mind racing furiously. She had to go find Jed to warn him! Listening carefully, she heard Carl telling Potter to get himself ready if he spotted Jed in the Cattleman. Then the door closed, and a second later Carl reappeared in the bedroom doorway.

'You heard it all, didn't you,' he told her, his voice low, controlled.

She wanted to deny it, but she couldn't. Her driving anger—at herself as well as Carl—overcame her caution. 'Yes, damn you! I heard it! Every word!'

'And you want to stop me,' he said, moving into the bedroom.

She stood upright, her chin thrusting out defiantly. 'And I will! I'll tell Jed what you're planning. And if you go through with it, I'll go to Judge Rawlins!'

'You'll tell old Eli, will you.'

'Yes!'

'What the matter? You still soft on Jed? I thought it was over between you two.'

'It is. Thanks to you! But that don't make what you're going to do right.'

Carl smiled at Jenny. It was more of a grimace than a smile, and as Jenny looked into Carl's face, she shuddered. 'It don't matter none if it's right or not, Jenny,' he told her softly. 'It has to be done—to save the Lazy 8. And you aren't going to stop me.'

He reached out and grabbed her left wrist. So powerful was his grip that she was afraid her wrist would snap from the pressure. His fingers tightened. And again he smiled.

'Carl!' she gasped. 'My wrist! You're hurting me!'

He twisted his right hand, slowly, causing her to bend backward in an effort to relieve the awful pain in her wrist. When she started to cry out, he pushed her roughly and she went flying back onto the bed. Then he took out his six-gun.

'No, Carl,' she whispered, terrified. 'No? They'll hear the shot! You'll hang.'

'No, I won't,' he said, bringing the Colt down and around in a brutal swipe that caught her flush on the left side of her face. The barrel raked a wide furrow in her cheek as it snapped her head around, pulling her whole body with it. She was unconscious when her body came to rest.

153

She was lying on her side, one knee drawn up, a leg naked from the thigh down poking out from under the light blue nightdress she was wearing. Her face was covered by her thick hair, now spilling luxuriantly over her head like a dark blot in the dim light. He reached down and pulled her shouldered back. Her slack body responded easily to his force. He brushed the hair out of her eyes and looked down at her face. Leaning close, he inspected her with clinical detachment, then slapped her roughly a couple of times to bring her around.

Her eyes fluttered open, then stared in wide-eyed terror up at him.

Carl smiled. 'If I kill you,' he told her, 'I'll do it quietly, don't worry. They won't hang me if I do it right, and I will.'

'Please!' she cried. 'Don't ... don't hurt me! Don't hit me again!'

'I'll do worse if you don't stay right here for the rest of the night. Do you understand that?'

Her hand slowly raising to her swollen cheek, she nodded.

'Right here in this little shack that Jed rented for you. Don't try to warn him. There's nothing you can do for him. That clear?'

'Yes,' she whispered.

He stepped back, still watching her warily. She stared up at him wordlessly, her left hand still raised to the rapidly swelling welt on the side of her face. She had a curiously crooked look, as if all her features were now completely askew. And her eyes were wide and frightened. They reminded him of the eyes of a snared rabbit he had once stumbled upon and then casually shot.

He wondered if he should hit her again just to make sure, but the look in her eyes convinced him that she was completely cowed and would do as he said. He reached toward her. She shrank from him with a tiny cry. Chuckling, he took a corner of the bedspread and flung the blanket over her.

'Get some sleep,' he said. 'I'll be back in a little while. This shouldn't take long—not long at all.'

*   *   *

As Jed nursed his beer in the Cattleman and pondered what he had learned earlier that day at North Fork Pass, he wished very much that he still had his deputy around. Frank had had a nice way of just listening at times, reserving judgment until all the facts were in, and then kind of leading Jed to the proper assessment of what he had gathered. He sure as hell missed Frank, and that was a fact.

He lifted his stein and drank deep, as Doc Wynant entered, caught sight of Jed, and steered himself in Jed's direction. Jed was

155

glad to see him. He had found the doctor busy earlier and had asked him to meet Jed in the Cattleman later if he could.

'What a day!' Wynant said, as he collapsed wearily in the chair beside Jed.

He glanced up, caught the barkeep's eye, and held up one finger. The barkeep nodded and reached for a stein. As soon as the girl placed it down in front of him a moment later, Wynant raised it in a salute to Jed and swallowed a generous portion.

'Now, then,' he said, wiping the foam off his drooping mustache. 'What is this you want to see me about?'

'I don't know exactly. I guess I just want someone to listen to what I got, then help me sort it out.'

'Why me?'

'Because Frank is dead and because you're the one who told me about that fatal round, the one that entered Clayt from the rear. Hell, if you hadn't told me about that, this would all be a very simple exercise for me about now.'

'How so?'

'I would know for sure who killed Clayt.'

'And you don't now?'

'Not if what you told me is true.'

'It was that fourth bullet that killed Clayt,' Wynant said emphatically. 'And it came from behind.'

'And it came from a Winchester.'

'More than likely.'

'And that's what messes it all up.'

'I'm listening,' Wynant said, sipping his beer alertly.

'This is just between you and me right now. All right?'

'Between a doctor and his patient. Sure. Sacred trust and all that. My mouth is sealed. Now what the hell have you got?'

'Natalie Brewster told me she killed Clayt Durant.'

Jed had spoken this very softly, and as Wynant leaned closer to catch every word, his eyes grew wide in startled surprise. Then he looked around at the crowded, smoky interior of the saloon. The level of noise in the place was steady, with occasional barks of laughter from one of the tables in the rear or from the group at the far end of the bar. But not a patron had looked in the direction of Jed's table. No one had heard what Jed had just told the flabbergasted doctor.

Looking back at Jed, Wynant said, 'Christ, Jed. We shouldn't be talking about this in here!'

'Just keep your voice down.'

'How do you know this?'

'She told me. She also told me she will not admit this to anyone, will not testify in court.'

'Why did she do it?'

'Clayt tried to rape her.'

Wynant took out a crumpled handkerchief

157

and mopped his brow, glanced quickly around him, then looked back at Jed. 'I can understand that. Hell, a lot of bucks hereabouts been thinkin' of doin' the same thing. To maybe bring her down off her high horse.' Then he leaned suddenly forward. 'So what's your problem? You've solved it. She says she killed him, and she had a good reason.'

'It ain't that easy, not if what you maintain about that last fatal bullet is right.'

Wynant frowned. 'The Winchester, you mean.'

Jed nodded and picked up his stein. 'She said she took his six-gun and shot him with it. Clayt's six-gun. In her state at the time, I can imagine that easy enough. I can then see her dropping the gun and fleeing the place and riding hell-bent-for-leather back to the big house. But what I sure as hell can't see, Doc, is her going outside the shack and with Clayt lying on his stomach in a pool of blood, firing at him once more in the back with a Winchester. It just don't make sense. Natalie was defending herself from Clayt. Once she had stopped him, she would have no stomach for returning to shoot him in the back.' Jed picked up his glass of beer and drained it.

'You got a point, all right,' Wynant admitted. 'It don't ring true, her coming back to do something like that. So what you're saying is she shot Clayt, but she wasn't the one who killed him.'

'That's what I'm saying. Even though Natalie is convinced she killed Clayt, she and no one else. You saw how she reacted to the lynching of Sukeforth.'

'I wasn't there, thank God, but I heard about it.'

'I'm going to go back to the Lazy 8 and get her statement to clear Sukeforth,' Jed said, 'but there's a murderer still loose around here, and I haven't the slimmest chance of catching him.' Jed glanced over at the bar, caught the barkeep's eye, and held up one finger. He looked back at Wynant. 'And that don't make me feel good at all.'

'I guess I don't blame you.' Wynant looked shrewdly at Jed. 'Why not let it go at that, then? You know Natalie didn't kill him, that it was someone else. So why pester her for a statement? Right about now I figure she's suffered enough.'

'She's suffered too damn much is what I'm thinking. When I get her statement, I'm going to make it plain to her that I don't think it was her bullets that killed Clayt. More than likely, if Clayt hadn't been shot again, Clyde Sukeforth would have found him and been able to save his life.'

'All right. Tell her that. But why get the statement then?'

'So I can go after Harlow and that son of his. So this whole town, this entire countryside, will know that Harlow Brewster and his son hanged an innocent man. It might go a long way toward pulling that sonofabitch's teeth—and at the same time cool off those nesters. They're gathering right now in North Creek Pass. They're armed and they are ready to kill. Range wars are always ugly, but this one will be a real shocker, I'm thinking.'

Jed looked up as he finished speaking. The girl bringing his beer had been intercepted before she reached his table. Carl Brewster, a devilish smile on his face, took the stein of beer from the girl, patted her lightly on the backside, then continued with it to Jed's table. Jed was surprised. He had not seen Carl enter the Cattleman.

'Mind if I join you?' Carl asked Jed.

'Yes,' Jed said.

His reply was uttered in a quiet, but resonant, voice that carried far in the suddenly silent saloon. It was then that Jed realized that every eye in the place was looking at his table, watching this confrontation with alert eagerness.

'You won't drink with me, Sheriff?'

'I'd sooner drink with a skunk,' Jed replied easily.

Carl hurled the contents of the stein into Jed's eyes. His action was so swift that Jed had no time to protect his eyes from the drink, and in his effort to do so, he toppled

160

backward, bringing the chair over with him. As he hit the floor, he started to claw blindly for his Colt. It was in his right hand, clear of the leather, but he was still having some difficulty seeing clearly. He blinked his eyes frantically and looked up at Carl's grinning face. He frowned. Carl had not drawn his six-gun. Abruptly, the young man strode forward and kicked Jed's weapon from his hand.

As it went clattering over the floor, Carl turned his back on Jed and walked toward the batwings. Before he pushed through them, he glanced back at Jed, who was now standing, furious, beside his overturned chair.

'I'll be waiting outside, Sheriff,' Carl said. 'If you're yellow, you'll stay in here. If you're a damned fool, you'll come out after me.'

Then he vanished through the batwings.

In the ensuing silence, the only sound was the soft beat of the small doors as they closed behind Carl. Silently, the tense crowd watched Jed, alert to see if he would accept Carl's challenge. They'd never seen a man called out before; their eyes were alight with excitement.

'What are you going to do?' asked Wynant softly, as he reached up and gently took Jed's arm. 'He's gone plum crazy, looks like.'

'He's calling me out, I'm going out,' Jed replied softly.

'That's a fool thing to do, and you know it.

161

He won't be alone, not that one!'

There was a murmur of agreement to that sentiment, and at once the crowd inside the Cattleman gained a voice. Everyone started to talk at the same time, it seemed. The sudden hubbub was almost comical as more than half the saloon's patrons rushed to the bar to order a drink. Jed turned and strode back to the wall and picked up his six-gun.

As he examined the weapon carefully and checked the cylinders, the place quieted again. When he dropped the Colt back into his holster, the silence was broken by a single husky voice. 'Go get the sonofabitch, Sheriff. He's got it coming!'

A chorus of shouts greeted that sentiment. Everyone, it seemed, agreed. With a slight smile, Jed nodded to the patrons, brushed past the very concerned Wynant, and stepped through the batwings. He heard chairs scraping and feet shuffling hurriedly to the door and windows as everyone inside rushed to catch a glimpse of the action.

Carl was right. Jed reflected ironically as he paused on the boardwalk outside the saloon. He was a damned fool. And Wynant was correct too when he said that Carl would not be alone. But it didn't matter. This had been building a long time between him and Carl. Only Jed's respect for what his badge stood for had kept him from going after Carl. Now Carl had let him off the hook.

He had made it perfectly legal for Jed to kill him.

Carl appeared out of the shadows beside the hotel. He took a few strides toward Jed, his Colt in his hand, then stopped, feet wide, and waited. Jed took out his own weapon, left the boardwalk, and started toward Carl. The distance was too great for either of them to chance a shot. Jed passed the barber shop and saw the faces of a boy and his father peering out at him through the plate glass window. Jed was always amazed at how quickly news of a shoot-out could travel through a town.

Carl went down on one knee, brought up his Colt and steadying it with both hands, fired at Jed. The round kicked up dirt a few feet in front of Jed, then tumbled off to rattle among some barrels sitting in front of Gus Hiram's general store.

Jed kept on walking. He intended to make sure before he fired.

The streets were deserted. Only a few skittish horses remained at the tie rails. The flaring street lamps shut out the night sky and cast a bright, lurid glow over the street and the fronts of the buildings, creating pools of light and sharply etched shadows. Recalling Wynant's warning, Jed peered carefully into each shadowy doorway and alley that he passed.

Still down on one knee, Carl fired a second time. Jed heard the bullet whisper past him a

163

few feet over his head. To his mild surprise, he did not hear it strike anything behind him. Jed kept going, his Colt up and ready now. When he could make out the buttons on Carl's blue cotton shirt, he cocked the gun.

Carl scrambled to his feet, threw a hasty shot at Jed, then bolted toward the alley he emerged from earlier. At once Jed took after him. The sight of his quarry fleeing before him caused a wild exultancy to flow through him. He almost fired a careless round after Carl as the rancher's son disappeared into the alley beside the hotel.

He didn't, however, and pulled up sharply just outside the alley, flattening himself against the hotel wall. This would be a good place for Carl to spring a surprise. He waited until his eyes were able to pick out the features of the alley to his satisfaction. The alley was clear for the most part, with nothing along either wall except a pile of crates near the hotel's rear entrance.

He glanced up at the hotel's windows. They were all closed. He would be able to hear one opening if Carl had a confederate—Phil Potter, say—hidden inside the hotel. Jed looked back at the crates, studied them for a while, then slowly, carefully raised his six-gun. His first shot brought no response. He saw a splinter of wood leap skyward and that was all. He fired a second time, putting the shot closer to the back of the pile, near the wall.

The crates seemed to explode as Carl leaped out from behind them and raced down the alley. Jed left the hotel wall, his eyes gleaming, and started after Carl. He had gone no more than a stride when he heard running footsteps behind him and a kind of sobbing cry. Hauling up, he turned in time to see a distraught Jenny rushing into the alley mouth after him.

There was something wrong with her face. She was holding it as she ran, and with the other hand she was pointing up at the hotel balcony. At once he understood. At the same time that he swung his Colt up toward the balcony—and the dim figure he saw crouched there—a terrific blast ruptured the darkness of the alley. For a second Jed was blinded by the shotgun's charge—and then he tumbled backward, Jenny's body slamming into him with such force that he went down with her on top of him just as the bushwhacker fired the second barrel down on them from the balcony.

He felt the buckshot's impact through Jenny's body. Her bone and sinew, covering him solidly, seemed to dissolve under the force of this second onslaught. He rolled out from under Jenny's torn frame and fired up repeatedly at the shadowy figure crouched just behind the balcony's rail. He saw his second round whip the man around. His third shot sent him reeling backward out of sight.

He was on his feet then, racing back into the street. He turned and looked up at the balcony. Someone was stumbling crookedly across the porch roof, carrying a shotgun. It could have been Phil Potter from his build, Jed realized as he hauled up, aimed carefully, and sent a shot into him. The fellow lost all forward momentum and collapsed woodenly down onto the porch roof, vanishing from sight.

Jed turned and raced back into the alley. Since he was always careful to rest the hammer on an empty chamber, he had only one round left in his revolver. But this did not matter. The fury that galvanized him left no room for caution. He traversed the alley swiftly and broke into the next street in time to see Carl swinging aboard his mount. Pulling up hastily, Jed steadied his gun with his left hand and squeezed off a shot. But even as the .45's powerful recoil sent the butt snapping into his palm, Carl was well out of range.

It was then that Jed collapsed forward as his right leg abruptly lost all power to sustain him. Sprawling crookedly in the dust, he put his hand down to grab at his leg and felt only the warm, heavy slickness of his own blood. He struggled to rise. It was suddenly more important than life itself that he get back to Jenny. He had something he had to tell her.

For a moment he was on his feet, dimly aware of townspeople pouring out of the alley toward him.

And then he was plunging once more to the ground, only this time he fell right on through it into bottomless darkness...

CHAPTER TEN

The news of the shoot-out in Sundown—and its fatal consequences—spread to the state capital within two days. At once, the opposition party in the legislature demanded the attorney-general send in U.S. marshals to investigate. The state's most influential newspaper, meanwhile, rehashed the earlier lynching in great detail, making much of the fact that events in Sundown were apparently going from bad to worse while the governor did nothing to stem the tide of increasing lawlessness.

The governor wisely made no public comment on the matter, and by the end of that week the newspaper was full of news items and editorials concerning the Chinese Problem, as it urged the passage of laws designed to prevent Chinese scabs from being pressed into service as strike breakers. This state of affairs, if allowed to continue, would throw honest white men out of work throughout the West, a threat dire enough to overturn the Republic.

Only then did the governor send a trusted aide to warn Harlow Brewster. The fellow took the train to Sundown, hired a trap at the livery stable, and paid a short visit to the Lazy 8. He returned as unobtrusively as he had come.

The message he brought to Harlow from the governor was short and to the point: The governor did not need to know the details of either the lynching or the gunfight in Sundown. But until the federal court rendered its judgment concerning the disposition of the North Basin lands, Brewster was to do nothing to arouse the settlers and he was to keep his riders out of Sundown. Otherwise, the attorney-general would be instructed to conduct a full investigation of not only the events leading up to the lynching, but the shoot-out, as well.

*　　　*　　　*

Jed almost stumbled as he reached out with both hands for the upholstered chair Rose had placed in front of the window. Swinging himself around with the skill that came with long practice, he sat down heavily, then glanced up at Rose, grinning.

'How's that?'

'You've been practising.'

'I'll be out of here before the end of the week. I'm still unsteady, but two days ago, I couldn't sit up on the edge of the bed without getting dizzy.'

'You're pushing it, Jed.'

'I'm not doing anyone any good up here.'

'Yes, you are,' she said softly, her pale face flushing slightly.

'You know what I mean, Rose,' he said gently.

'Things are quiet, very quiet. Relax. You can take all the time you need. You lost a great deal of blood, and besides, Doc Wynant insists there's still some buckshot left in your thigh.'

Jed grinned uneasily. 'Oh, the buck is still in there, all right. I know that. But lying on my back is not going to help much to get rid of it.'

Rose shrugged and moved close to him. She placed a hand on his shoulder as she looked past him down at the quiet street. He placed his hand on hers.

'You've been very good to me, Rose. It's more than I deserve.'

She laughed. 'I know that.'

'I only come to you when I'm banged up, or crippled.'

'At least you know where to come. The door's always open, Jed.'

'Thanks, Rose.'

'Why don't you quit? Let Brewster and the

nesters fight it out. They will anyway, you know.'

'And do what? Become your chief bouncer?'

'I don't have to keep a house for the rest of my life.'

'I'm a county sheriff, Rose. I don't know much else. It's too late now for either of us to change our spots.'

Rose said nothing for a while. Then she sighed. 'I suppose you're right,' she admitted, after a while. 'You sound so sensible all of a sudden. I think I liked you better when you were . . . what I called you: a romantic fool.'

'We *do* have to grow up, don't we?'

She patted him on the shoulder. 'Yes,' she said. 'I am afraid we do, at that.' She kissed him lightly on the cheek. 'I have to awaken the girls,' she said. 'It's almost noon. Enjoy the sun.'

As soon as she was gone, he turned his face and let the sun warm him. He felt like a flower that had just poked its head up in the morning after a long, wet night. He was alive. And it felt good to be alive. For a while there, with his life's blood pouring from him in great, throbbing gouts, he had been almost certain that it was over—and, swept along on a tide of self-pity and bitterness, he had thought of Jenny and wept.

He thought of her now and felt only an arousing, transfiguring anger. It charged him

170

with purpose and was what had forced him off his bed the night before and started him on his lonely, sweat-popping struggle to move upright on his two legs again. Rose, busy downstairs, had not known of his effort and so Jed had been free to sprawl helplessly to the floor over and over again until at last, sometime before dawn, he had made it from the bed to the window and back again twice before he collapsed, exhausted, on the bed.

Rose was right, of course. Though it was quiet now, Harlow Brewster and the nesters would soon be fighting it out. More than once this past week, Jed had gone over in his mind what Will Sukeforth had told him. And then Jed had seen the new arrivals, all of them hard and bitter, seemingly, and each one armed. Will meant what he said. As he reminded Jed, he had lost his father. There wasn't much else that he could lose to match that loss.

Thinking of Jenny, Jed understood perfectly Will Sukeforth's state of mind.

He turned his head and looked across the room at the closed door. It was twice the distance of the bed, he realized. He could use the bedposts for support the first couple of times. And by sundown he wouldn't be needing them at all.

Slowly, carefully, his face grim with resolve, Jed pushed himself out of the armchair and started toward the door. He just made it to the bed, hung on to the bedpost for a moment, then pushed off resolutely for the door.

★   ★   ★

Will Sukeforth reined in the large, ungainly horse he was astride. He was uncomfortable in the saddle, but he paid that no attention as he looked down and waited for Zeke Summerworth to thread his way down the gully ahead of his small band of riders. Once Summerworth and the others broke into the swale, Will raised his Winchester skyward and pumped two quick shots into the night.

Spreading out along the flanks of the big herd, Zeke's men began firing over the heads of the restless cattle. The valley floor beneath Will shook and the herd was off. All five hundred head on their feet and running as one animal. Will caught a glimpse of plunging backs in the bright moonlight and heard the sound of clicking horns as they reached the sloping sides of the narrow valley and made the turn. Peering into the night, he saw the crazed animals milling about, their heads jammed, some with their heads locked. Others were rearing up and riding over others—the mass of them gleaming in the moonlight like a bristling nest of snakes.

And then, in an instant it seemed, the flow of animals straightened, the plunging backs achieved a kind of steady, driving momentum, and the herd swept out of sight behind the shouldering rampart of rock that marked the valley's entrance.

Will sat his horse a moment longer to watch Zeke and his men disappear after the herd. Then he hauled his mount around and rode back off the bluff toward a campfire gleaming in among the pines. A moment later, the two night guards who had been posted to watch the Barbed Y's herd and who were now standing sullenly under Nathanial Tanner's Hawken, looked bleakly up at Will as he rode into the circle of light thrown by the campfire.

They had been caught with their britches down, and they knew it.

Will did not dismount. He looked at Tanner. 'You got their guns?'

Tanner nodded and patted his belt. Looking closer, Will saw the two butts protruding above Tanner's belt line.

Will looked back at the two men. 'Tell Yank Walsh this night is only the beginning. The next herd we rimrock of his won't be this small.'

The taller of the two cowhands straightened angrily. 'You mean you just rimrocked all them beeves?'

'What did you expect us to do with them? There's too many there to eat. They should be at the bottom of Splitrock Canyon by now,

I'd say.'

'You sonofabitch!' the man gasped.

Will considered the man for a long moment, then shrugged. His companion, he noted, was keeping his mouth shut. There was something about this other one that sounded an alarm deep within Will. Frowning, he looked back at the fellow who had just called him a sonofabitch.

'It don't matter what I am now, mister. Just give that message to Yank. And tell him he can thank Harlow Brewster for this. Tell him he's going to have to choose between following Brewster and losing a hell of lot more than his beef—or cutting loose of Brewster. It's his choice. Brewster or us. You think you can make that clear to him?'

The man nodded unhappily. 'How you gonna know which he chooses?'

'What's your name?'

'Tim Foley.'

'Tim, you tell your boss to send you to the North Fork Pass if he wants to call us off—on those terms I just mentioned. If you don't show in a couple of days, I'll know what his answer is.'

'You took our horses.'

'That's right. You're both going to have to walk back to the ranch.'

Both men looked stricken at this. And for the first time the other cowpoke turned to face Will directly, but his courage vanished

174

when his eyes met Will's and he said nothing.
But that single harsh glance was enough.

Now Will knew who he was.

He nudged his horse closer to the man.
'What's your name?'

'Scanlon. Art Scanlon.'

'Scanlon, ain't you one of the men who was
helping pull some of my Pa's belongings out
of our burning cabin?'

The fellow swallowed unhappily. 'Sure,' he
admitted. 'I helped. We didn't want to see all
your stuff burn up.'

'You were only trying to help.'

'That's right.'

'You weren't doing it willingly, as I
remember.'

'Well, hell—them flames was getting pretty
hot.' The fellow tried to smile apologetically.

'I remember you,' Will said, slowly
drawing his own six-gun, 'because you were
the one who prevented my sister Sherry from
taking her doll from the burning cabin. She
broke past you with it in her hand and
accidentally knocked you to one side. You
were furious with her. You snatched the doll
away from her and tossed it into the flames.
Yes, I remember you.'

The man's face had gone chalk white. His
eyes, as he stared at the revolver in Will's
hand, became like two spreading holes in his
face. 'Jesus!' he stammered. 'I didn't mean
nothin'. I was just nervous. I didn't know

175

what I was doing!'

'Sherry loved that doll. I made it for her. Out of cornstalks and flour sacks. When she was no bigger than a minute.'

Will cocked and fired at Scanlon. The round printed a neat hole in Scanlon's shirt from just under his breast pocket. Scanlon staggered back, but did not go down. Will cocked and fired a second time and the right side of Scanlon's face vanished. The man spun violently about and fell across the campfire. His narrow waist was enveloped by the leaping flames, but Scanlon rested in the fire without moving. The smell of burning cloth filled the air.

Both Tanner and Tim Foley hurriedly dragged Scanlon out of the fire and rolled him over. Foley gasped as Tanner looked up at Will.

'My God, Will! He's a dead man! You've taken a life!'

'Pa's dead, ain't he?'

'Yes, but . . . !'

'What's that you been telling us, Preacher? An eye for an eye and a tooth for a tooth. Ain't that what you been saying?'

Tanner straightened as he let Scanlon drop loosely at his feet and, stroking his long beard, looked back up at Will with suddenly gleaming eyes. 'Yes, Will! An eye for an eye and a tooth for a tooth! Vengeance is mine, saith the Lord!'

'And we are the instruments of the Lord's vengeance!'

'Yes, Will!'

Will looked back at Tim Foley. 'Add this to your report to Yank Walsh, Foley. Tell him that with the sheriff out of it now, we're going to play according to Brewster's rules. We can use a rope too. And bullets.'

In no condition to offer argument, the cowpoke simply nodded, then pointed down at Scanlon's body. 'What about Art?'

'Leave him for the buzzards. Get going. Now.'

When he hesitated, Tanner nudged him back out of the circle of light with two quick, vicious pokes with the barrel of his Hawken. Foley stumbled once, then turned and fled through the pines.

★　　　★　　　★

Harlow Brewster, sunk deep into his leather armchair, was dozing fitfully. Haunting, fragmented scenes from his life in Texas drew him deeper into sleep. He felt the solidity of his armchair falling away from him. He was riding hard across a bright meadowland with Carl on his pony, still far ahead of him, barely visible in the morning light. Harlow felt an intolerable, aching sense of loss and tried to call out to his boy. But the cry caught in his throat and in that instant Carl vanished...

'Pa!'

Harlow opened his eyes, startled. Carl had his hand on his shoulder and was shaking him. 'Must have dozed off,' Harlow muttered. That knifing sense of loss he had felt in the dream still clung to him—stronger than ever, as if he were still in the dream. Yet here was Carl, close enough to touch, leaning down and peering anxiously at him.

'It's Yank Walsh, Pa. He just rode in with two of his riders. He's waitin' outside on his horse. He won't speak to me. Says he wants to see you.'

Harlow got slowly to his feet. 'I could use some coffee,' he said. 'Got any idea what Yank wants?'

'Well, he ain't got good news. I can tell from the look of him. But then he's no better than an old woman. Some nester probably said boo to him.'

Harlow looked at his son. There was a pinched, mean look about his eyes that Harlow did not like. Oh, God, he thought. There's *nothing* about him I like. The thought alarmed him, frightened him, it was so disloyal. He shook it off as he had the dream, and squaring his shoulders, he left the room ahead of Carl, told Alice he wanted fresh coffee for his guests, then strode out onto the porch.

It was close to dusk. The three riders looked weary. Their hats, eyebrows, and

178

shoulders were covered with dust. 'Light and rest a spell,' Harlow told Yank and his men. He smiled. 'You've had a long ride.'

Yank appeared to be too unhappy to accept the invitation. At the same time he didn't have the steel to refuse such an offer from Harlow Brewster. He said something to his riders and then wearily dismounted, as usual, his broad beam giving him some difficulty. Puffing like a woman, he handed the reins of his horse to one of his men and walked up onto the porch as the two turned their mounts and headed for the cookshack, evidently where Yank had told them to go. It was, Harlow remembered, Yank's way of handling his men. He didn't believe it proper for the hands to sit down at the same table with the owner. Destroyed the men's respect for him.

'We got fresh coffee on,' said Harlow, moving into the house with Yank. Carl stuck close behind them and closed the door after them as they headed for the dining room.

'This ain't a social call, Harlow,' Yank said, as he collapsed wearily into a chair at the long dining room table and placed his dust-laden hat down on the gleaming, polished mahogany surface. He blinked owlishly across at Harlow and waited as Alice brought in the coffee on a silver tray.

Sipping his coffee, Harlow leaned back, aware of his son beside him staring intently at Yank. 'So why did you come then?' he asked.

179

'We've got trouble, Harlow.'

Harlow took a deep breath. 'I know that, Yank. That's all we've had since those nesters got the idea they could squat in the North Basin. Now, what's eatin' at you this time? I told you. We got to wait until the courts give their decision, and that's just what we're going to do. Waitin' should suit you fine.'

'Maybe we're waiting. Maybe we got our tails curled under our asses, but not them settlers! They've done murdered my man, Art Scanlon—and rimrocked one of my herds!'

Harlow leaned suddenly forward, almost spilling his coffee. 'They *what?*'

'You heard what I said, Harlow. I didn't make that up. Tim Foley walked in this afternoon with the story. I sent riders to Splitrock Canyon, and it's true. Every word. And that ain't all. A rider from the Flying Seven rode in just as I was leaving to come here. Nesters raided last night and burned them out. A couple of men almost got trapped in the bunkhouse, and the big house is gutted. There's one stable left, and that's all.'

Harlow did not know what to say. It was Carl who spoke, his voice urgent. 'Who's leading them?'

'Clyde Sukeforth's son. Will. You remember the one. Tim said he shot and killed Art because Art was one of them took part in the burning of his cabin. Vengeance.

180

He's out for vengeance, Harlow. He told Tim that with Jed out of it, it was your rules now. The rope and the gun, he said. He's gone mad, I tell you.'

As Harlow listened to Yank, hope blazed anew in his gut. And when the man had finished, Harlow slammed his fist down on the table with a force that almost upset the cream pitcher on the silver tray. 'He's made the first move, then! We'll take them now, every mother's son of them! The fat's in the fire and they're the ones responsible this time. The governor can't come down on us after this! Hell!' he cried, looking at Carl almost joyously. 'We have no choice! We've got to defend ourselves!'

But when Harlow looked back at Yank, he saw the man shaking his head gloomily. 'No,' he said. 'I'm out of it, Harlow. I don't want any more trouble. I've already sent Tim to tell Will Sukeforth that I won't oppose him or any of his settlers if they try to stake out homesteads in the North Basin.'

'You *what?*'

'You heard me, Harlow,' the man said, slowly laboriously pushing himself to his feet. He had not touched the coffee set before him. 'I'm out of it. If you want to stop them, you'll have to do without the Barbed Y.'

Harlow sat back in his chair, his dark, piercing eyes regarding Yank Walsh coldly, but without rancor. 'If you haven't the

181

stomach for this business, Yank, you shouldn't be in it. All right then. We'll just have to pull your chestnuts out of the fire along with our own.'

Yank frowned unhappily. 'It ain't just the Barbed Y that's pulling out. The Flying 7's finished too. Wiped out. Flynn's already given his men their wages.'

'I can understand that,' Harlow said unhappily. 'From what you said, his men don't even have a place to sleep now. Right?'

'That's about it, Harlow.'

'So that leaves just the Lazy 8 and the Spur. I better send a rider to warn him.'

'I already done that, Harlow.' Reaching over, Yank lifted his hat from the table and clapped it back onto his head. 'Sorry about this, Harlow,' he said.

Without responding, Harlow got up from the table and walked Yank to the door, Carl at his side. Moving out onto the veranda, Yank waved his men over. They left the cluster of Lazy 8 hands they were visiting with in front of the cookshack and brought Yank his horse. Once aboard his mount, Yank waved solemnly to Harlow and Carl, then led his men from the compound at a brisk trot.

'It's just as well,' said Carl meanly. 'We don't need that yellowbelly. He never had the stomach for this business, anyway.'

Harlow nodded grimly. 'Maybe you're
182

right, Carl. But right now we've got work to do. Tell the men to get their mounts ready. We've got some hard riding ahead of us. My feeling is that Pete Antell is next on Sukeforth's list. I want to get there before the nesters do. Right now, we need Pete's riders at our back.'

'How come you think Sukeforth will go for the Spur before us?'

'Don't you see, Carl? He's stripping away our support. And when he's done that, then he'll come for us.'

'The sonofabitch.'

'Yes. He's that. Another thing, select your best men to stay behind to guard the compound and send at least four men to round up our stock in the north pasture and haze them onto the south flats with the rest. And after that, they're to keep their eyes open. As soon as we get back from the Spur, we'll reinforce them.'

Carl nodded and strode off the porch in the direction of the bunkhouse.

Harlow was turning around to go back in when Natalie appeared in the doorway. A streak of crimson light from the fading sun caught her full in the face—and in that instant he saw what these past few days had done to the brave, confident daughter he had once taken such pride in beholding. Her eyes were glazed, the flesh beneath them inflamed from crying, and her nose pinched and worn.

'Wasn't that Yank Walsh who just rode out, Pa?'

'Yes, Natalie, it was,' Harlow said, moving into the doorway and placing an arm on her shoulder. As he walked with her into the parlor, he was shocked to feel under his palm the sharp, gaunt outline of her shoulder bone. It was almost as if she were wasting away before his eyes.

Damn the governor, he thought bitterly. Had that milksop not shackled him this past week, he might have been able to clear out that nest of vipers before they could have gathered behind Sukeforth. Not until they were gone—each and every one of them—could this land of his breathe again—and Natalie begin to put all this behind her.

He felt a deep pang of guilt that he had not noticed before this what had been happening to his daughter, how deeply she had been affected.

'What did Yank want?' she asked, as she slipped like a wraith into the corner of the sofa and tucked her feet under her. She was wearing her blue housecoat, the one with the lace at her throat and along the hem. Worn pink slippers covered her feet.

'Bad news, I'm afraid.'

Natalie said nothing, but her pale face grew even grayer. 'Tell me,' she said.

Harlow told her all of what Yank had told

184

them, and when he had finished, he leaned back and watched her carefully. He was surprised and pleased to see a spark of indignation flashing in her eyes.

'They burned that beautiful house? The one that Emma and Sandy planned for so long? And all those beautiful curtains, the ones Emma and I sewed on for so many hours . . . !'

'According to Yank, the big house was gutted. There's no telling what they were able to save.'

'That's dreadful,' Natalie said softly, an edge to her voice Harlow had not heard in a long time. 'We've got to fight them!'

He smiled at his daughter, immensely relieved. 'And that is what we're going to do, Natalie. I just sent Carl out to get the boys ready to ride.'

'I'm coming too!'

'If you think you're up to it. But frankly, Natalie, I wish you'd stay here and rest up. You look kind of peaked, if you don't mind my saying so.'

'I don't feel peaked,' she said, her head back and her chin thrusting out. 'I feel angry. Very angry! That was a beautiful house!'

At that moment Harlow heard Carl hurrying into the house. He turned as his son appeared in the archway leading from the next room. Carl's face was set angrily, his eyes sullen.

185

'What is it, Carl?' Harlow asked. 'What's wrong?'

'You better speak to John, Pa. I'm afraid if I try, I might hurt the sonofabitch.'

Harlow frowned with sudden, overwhelming concern. Big John was the cook and had served for years as the unofficial spokesman for the hands. It was Clayt's inability to deal with John that had made Harlow realize Clayt would never really be able to run this ranch in Harlow's stead. If John was out there now waiting for him, there was trouble—big trouble—with the hands.

And at once he knew what it was.

'They're losing their stomach for this business, are they?' Harlow asked Carl.

'Maybe you can talk some sense into them,' Carl said, nodding.

Harlow brushed past Carl and hurried through the house and out onto the veranda. All the men were standing unhappily together in front of the big house, each one with his hat in his hand. Closest to the house stood Big John. The features of his men were not easy to distinguish in the gathering dusk, but from the slant to their shoulders and the angle of their heads, he could feel their unhappy but dogged resoluteness.

'What is this, John?' Harlow demanded. 'I sent Carl to get the men mounted up.'

Big John straightened up and squared his

186

shoulders. 'The men asked me to tell you they weren't going after them nesters any more.'

'Why? In heaven's name, why? Them nesters is out to destroy us all!'

Big John shifted unhappily, but the expression on his big, fleshy face remained resolute. 'No more, Mr. Brewster. They had enough.'

'Have they heard,' Harlow said, 'what them nesters did to Art Scanlon? Shot him down in cold blood! Since when are you men going to take that from sodbusters?'

Big John's response was sharp and came so swiftly that Harlow realized in that instant how primed his men were for this moment: 'We figure that after what Carl did to that girl of his and Jed Sanford, we ain't got a leg to stand on. Them nesters is just fighting fire with fire, the way we look at it.'

Both Carl and Natalie had joined Harlow on the veranda by this time. Harlow heard Carl suck in his breath angrily when Big John spoke of the shooting of Jenny La Rue and the sheriff. To his credit, however, Carl kept his mouth shut.

'We ain't going to beg you men to stay on,' said Harlow doggedly, a note of desperation creeping into his voice despite everything he could do to conceal his feelings. 'But the Lazy 8 has been a good brand to ride for over the years. It has always treated its men fairly and seen to it that they were fed by the best damned cook in the territory. We need you now to stamp out them nesters. We can't let them rip this land up and then string their barbed wire without a fight!'

There was some muttering from the now dark ranks of men behind Big John. The cook cleared his throat. 'It don't seem like we got much choice,' the big man said sorrowfully. 'There's been a lot of killing, and it ain't done no good. It's a war, Mr. Brewster, but we don't want to fight in it no more.'

At that, there was a solid grunt of assent from the men behind John. He had put in words precisely what they felt. Harlow knew then that he was licked, that no further words of his could bring these men around. It felt as if the bottom had dropped out of his world, and perhaps it had. He had taken his men's loyalty for granted. To see it evaporate like this was frightening. He felt suddenly vulnerable.

And the moment he became aware of that feeling he was consumed with a bitter, galling fury. He turned to Carl.

'Give them their time—all of them. Each man can take a mount from his string. I want them off this ranch by midnight.'

Then he hurried past Natalie into the house, scalding tears of disappointment and loss coursing down his rough cheeks.

CHAPTER ELEVEN

As Jed rode back down the street toward the livery stable, he was aware of how good it felt to be out of Rose's care finally.

It wasn't that she hadn't been wonderfully considerate and attentive. The thing was he thought he understood now why a canary would often stop singing. The cage might be cleaned out regularly and the bird well fed, but no living creature feels like singing through bars, no matter how sweet and yielding those bars might be at times.

Jed left his horse at the livery and walked back up the street to the Cattleman. The walk tired him surprisingly, but he made sure he entered the Cattleman without a trace of a limp. He paused a moment in front of the batwings, then caught sight of Eli and Doc Wynant at a table in the back. He joined them.

'Heard the latest?' Wynant asked, as Jed settled gratefully into a chair.

'Just rode in. Went clear to the Dusty and back. Fill me in.'

'Pete Antell's thrown in with Yank. They're making their peace with Sukeforth.'

'That's hard to believe.'

'Hell, the Spur lost five hundred head of cattle the same way Yank Walsh did.

Sukeforth's gone plumb crazy, Jed. With Brewster's hands gone, there's nothing now to stop him. Pete knew that. He had no choice.'

The judge shook his head. 'I can see the litigation now. It will extend from here to the capital and back. It's open warfare, Jed. But who's to blame. Like kids in a schoolyard. One starts pushing and the other pushes back. And then the teacher runs over and tries to establish blame. You know what that's like.'

Jed nodded grimly, caught the eye of the barkeep and held up one finger. As the barkeep drew his beer, Jed looked back to the table in time to see a nervous cowpoke, his stein in his hand, drawing up beside the table. He was looking at Jed.

'You still the sheriff, Jed?' the cowpoke asked nervously.

A slight smile broke Jed's pale, somewhat gaunt face. Then he looked around the table at Wynant and the judge. 'What do you think, men?'

The judge looked up at the cowpoke. 'Sure. Jed's still the sheriff.'

'He's a mite worn around the edges,' added Doc Wynant, with a wink at Jed. 'But no one's taken that badge away from him yet.'

'Then I'd like to talk to him,' said the man.

'Sit down,' Jed told him, reaching over with one hand and pulling out a chair.

The fellow sat down hastily. 'I'm Tim Foley,' he told Jed. 'I seen a murder, Sheriff. Straight out. I was a witness.'

Jed's beer was brought to the table by one of the girls. She wouldn't take payment. Jed thanked her and looked back at Foley. 'Why don't you try that again, Foley. A little slower this time. Start at the beginning.'

Foley tried to relate what he had witnessed quite calmly. But by the time he had finished describing Will Sukeforth's murder of Art Scanlon, the words were tumbling out of his mouth in a rush. When the cowpoke had finished, he leaned back. It was clear the brutal killing he had witnessed still haunted him. In a somber voice, he said, 'I had no choice. I had to leave Art there for the buzzards.'

'That's right, Foley,' said the doctor gently. 'You had no choice. There was no sense in arguing with those men.'

'I heard about Scanlon's death,' said Jed. 'But no particulars. Will you testify to this in a court of law, Foley?'

'If you can bring that sonofabitch in, I will.'

'I'll bring him in.'

'That ain't all.'

Jed looked at Foley and waited.

Foley took a sip of his beer, then wiped his mouth and leaned closer to the three men. 'Will Sukeforth and his men are on their way

191

to the Lazy 8 now. I saw them riding out on my way in here. I kept out of sight until they was past, then I pounded leather to get here. I just rode in before you did, Sheriff.'

'Makes sense,' said Jed to Eli. 'He's stripped away Brewster's support. Now Brewster's out there alone—waiting. I'd feel bad for Harlow if I didn't know any better.' Jed glanced back at Foley.

'I need a deputy, Tim. You game?'

'Me?'

'Yes, you. You want me to stop Sukeforth, don't you.'

'Sure, but . . .'

'No buts. Yes or no.'

The man looked swiftly around the table. Each one looked back calmly, encouragingly. Foley nodded swiftly. 'All right,' he said.

'Good,' said Jed. Then he turned to Eli. 'Judge, I need warrants.'

'How many?'

'A bushel before this is over, but right now only two. One for Harlow Brewster and the other for Carl.'

'How soon do you need them?'

'Like yesterday. I need something to bargain with. If Sukeforth can believe I've taken Harlow and his son in, maybe he'll call off his dogs. I'm just playing for time. Later, we'll see about bringing Sukeforth in, himself.'

'These warrants, Jed. What's the charge?'

192

'Murder. Hanging an innocent man.'

'You know that for a fact, do you?'

'I know who killed Clayt Durant. And it wasn't Will Sukeforth's father.'

'You have proof of that?'

'Enough to satisfy me.'

The judge got to his feet. 'Meet me at my office in half an hour.'

As Eli hurried from the saloon, Wynant looked closely at Jed. 'You ain't going to do any hard riding, are you, Jed? That thigh of yours is still full of buckshot, and you don't look any too healthy.'

'I'm healthy enough. I told you. I just returned from a ride out to the Dusty and back. Thanks to your excellent care, Doctor, I'm as fit as a fiddle.'

'That someone just finished stomping on! Hell, Jed. You're in no condition.'

Ignoring Wynant, Jed turned his attention back to his new deputy. 'Come with me to my office and I'll swear you in. Then I got a job for you.'

'What's that?'

'Organize a posse. See if you can intercept Sukeforth and his nesters. If you do, tell them I've already got Harlow Brewster and his son in custody for the lynching of Clyde Sukeforth. If that don't stop them, tell them I'm calling in U.S. marshals. They won't have the chance of a snowball in hell of winning their case in federal courts if they

193

tangle with federal officers.'

Foley moistened his lips nervously. 'You think I can get up much of a posse around here for pulling Brewster's chestnuts out of the fire, Sheriff? Everyone knows what that son of his did to Jenny and you. And it was Brewster who lynched that nester and caused all this burning and killing.'

'It won't be easy, Tim, and that's a fact. So that's why I'm going on ahead. Do what you can. Now, let's get to my office.'

As Jed and Foley got up from the table to leave, Doc Wynant turned and looked with concern up at Jed. 'Go easy on that thigh, you crazy fool,' he warned. 'And good luck.'

'Thanks,' Jed said. 'I'll need it.'

★   ★   ★

Despite Wynant's advice, Jed had ridden for the past two hours and was finally topping a long rise that he knew would give him a clear view of the Lazy 8's ranch buildings when he caught movement well off to his right. He pulled up carefully, since by this time he was in considerable pain, and saw that the luck Wynant had wished him was not to be.

Streaking out of a patch of timber and heading directly for the rise was Sukeforth and his nesters. Jed was sure it was them, not the posse, because he could make out clearly not only the rake-thin Sukeforth, but at his side the preacher, his long snowy beard streaming out behind him as he rode. He did not know if they had spotted him yet, but he was anxious that they slow down so that he could intercept them. Pulling his six-gun from his holster, he pumped two quick shots into the air.

As the two powerful detonations echoed across the sloping meadowland, he saw Sukeforth and the preacher pull up momentarily, then start up again in his direction. With a grunt of satisfaction, Jed put his horse back down the slope to meet them.

They met below the ridge, Sukeforth and the preacher pulling up in front of him while the rest of the nesters formed a glowering semi-circle about him. They were a hard-looking crew, riding every kind of horse and outfitted in an odd motley of hats and coats, rifles, and shotguns. They seemed to have only one thing in common—bottled fury. It blazed out at Jed from every pair of eyes.

'Heard you was out of action, Sheriff,' said Will Sukeforth.

'Not quite, Will.'

'I waited, like I said I would—until you got your ass shot off, and then I moved. You got no complaints, Sheriff.'

'My ass ain't shot off.'

'Damned close to it, from what I hear.'

'It's a sore piece of meat, and that's a fact. Anyway, you've accomplished what you wanted. You've driven off Brewster's support. He's alone now, isolated. Go back to your families now, and let me take it from here.'

'You must be crazy, Sheriff,' broke in Tanner, his eyes wild with anticipation. 'There's no turning back now! It's time for the Final Judgment on that Scourge out of Hell! His time has come!'

Will leaned back in his saddle and nodded at Jed. 'The preacher's right, Sheriff. We ain't waitin' now. We got that sonofabitch and his cub right where we want him, and now we're goin' to squeeze him 'til all the piss and bile comes out.'

'Go back, Will. There's a posse on the way. You got your families to think about. You could all go to jail.'

'It's our families we're thinking of,' cried Zeke, nudging his horse alongside Will's. 'And as for prisons, what do you think that pass has been for us this past couple of months?'

'Yes,' snapped Will. 'And our jailer was Harlow Brewster—and the law.'

Jed slapped his saddle bag. 'I have warrants for both Harlow and his son. Let me serve them. I promise you, they'll both be in jail before this day is out.'

Will frowned. 'Warrants?'

'Yes.'

'Let me see them.'

Jed untied the saddle bag and withdrew the warrants. He glanced quickly at them himself, then handed them to Will Sukeforth. The man read both warrants swiftly, then allowed the preacher to read them also. He studied Jed closely, and when Tanner handed back the warrants, he gave them to Jed.

'And you're going to ride in there now and serve those warrants?'

Dropping the warrants back into his saddle bag, Jed nodded. 'That's why I've ridden out here. I was on my way to the Lazy 8 when I spotted your party.'

'If you try to serve them warrants, Brewster will kill you, Sheriff. Either he will, or that son of his. Hell, Carl's already tried that, hasn't he?'

'Yep. But I'm still here.'

Will Sukeforth studied Jed shrewdly for a moment. Then he glanced up the slope leading to the ridge, beyond which, he knew, lay Brewster's ranch. Jed followed his gaze, looking past the cottonwoods just below the ridge. For a moment he thought he saw movement in among the trees.

'Tell you what,' Will said. 'Maybe you could deputize me, Sheriff. Zeke and I—and maybe a few others. We could be your posse. Sure. We could help you serve them warrants.' He smiled coldly. 'Legally.'

Jed knew at once that he was in a bind. How could he refuse help that he so obviously needed? And yet, how could he accept that help without dooming Harlow and his son, and possibly Natalie? Will Sukeforth and his riders had no intention of helping Jed serve these warrants. But they would make an excellent excuse for getting safely within firing range of the Brewsters.

At that moment a rifle cracked from well above them, from the cottonwoods. Even as the echo rolled past them, Tanner uttered a muffled cry and slipped from his saddle. Another shot sounded and Jed felt his horse sag heavily beneath him. He tried to swing clear of the falling animal and almost managed it. And then, his foot caught under the cantle; he struck the ground heavily.

As Jed pulled himself free of the struggling animal, he saw Tanner, his face drawn in pain, being pulled back up into his saddle by Will Sukeforth, while the other riders poured up the flank of the hill toward the cottonwoods. A steady fire was issuing from the timber by this time, and as Jed scrambled to his feet with his six-gun drawn and started to limp up the slope after them, he saw first one and then another rider peel from his horse. With a mad, reckless disregard for their lives, the nesters continued to drive their mounts up the slope into the withering fire.

Jed found a riderless horse, stepped into its saddle, and spurred the animal up the slope after the nesters. They were nearing the timber by this time, firing blindly into the trees. The rifle fire coming from the cottonwoods ceased abruptly. On a hunch, Jed started to cut around the timber. As he neared the ridge, he saw a horseman break out of the timber on the other side. In a moment the rider had crossed the ridge and dropped to the other side, galloping swiftly toward the Lazy 8 far below.

It was Carl Brewster.

By this time the nesters were riding into the timber, still shooting at will, hoping to run down the bushwhacker. They had been too close to the cottonwoods to see Carl bolt from the far side of the timber.

Jed galloped toward the ridge, his six-gun out and ready, hoping to overtake Carl. He was not going to serve Carl a warrant this time. The shot that had killed his mount had come damned close to killing him. He was getting weary of serving as Carl Brewster's favorite target. Cresting the ridge, Jed heard a shout a hundred yards or so below him and saw Tanner—his incredible beard flowing behind him like a pennant—break from the timber on Carl's heels. Tanner was already closer to Carl than Jed and was cutting toward him at an angle.

Carl must have heard the pounding hooves

of the preacher's horse. He turned and flung a shot at his pursuer. He was lucky. The bullet slammed into Tanner's mount. As it went down, Tanner was thrown free. The preacher came down hard and should have stayed down, considering his earlier wound. But the man was up instantly, clawing his Hawken from the saddle sling of his downed horse. While Jed galloped swiftly closer to him, Tanner rested the Hawken's barrel on his dead horse's streaming rump and squeezed off a shot.

The gray Carl was riding suddenly pitched forward to its knees, throwing Carl over its head. Jed pounded past Tanner, and as Carl struggled groggily to his feet, his six-gun in his fist, Jed called out to him.

'Drop it, Carl!'

Instead, Carl raised his gun to fire. Jed fired first. The round caught Carl below his knee, snapping his leg out from under him. Barely visible in the tall grass, Carl cried out in sudden pain and began thrashing. By that time Jed had reached him. He dismounted swiftly and kicked Carl's revolver away from him. Then he bent to inspect Carl's wound. The bullet appeared to have missed the shin bone. Jed straightened. Reaching up to grab the pommel of his saddle for support, he watched Carl Brewster.

Glancing up at Jed, Carl smiled. It was more of a snarl than a smile. He stopped his agonized thrashing and said, 'Sonofabitch, Sheriff. You got more lives than a cat.'

That was all the time they had for conversation.

The ground shook under them as Will and the nesters galloped up. The riders milled about like crazed Indians, leaning away from their horses to get a better look at Carl. They were ominously silent, however. All Jed could hear was the horses' snorting and the riders' heavy breathing. But as Jed studied their grim faces, he knew that he had little need for Carl Brewster's warrant now.

A rope snaked out, settled over Carl's shoulders, then was yanked tight. It was Will Sukeforth's rope. Will hauled his horse around and galloped back through the ring of horsemen, dragging Carl along the ground behind him. The nesters parted to let Will through, then, with a shout, followed him back up the slope toward the ridge and the cottonwoods beyond.

*   *   *

Tanner was dead. They found him slumped behind his dead horse, his Hawken still clutched in his hands; his chest wound had been a fatal one, making all the more awesome his performance after receiving it. This, along with the fatal wounding of another nester, dampened considerably the pleasure Will Sukeforth, Zeke, and the others felt as they hauled Carl up into the tallest of the cottonwood trees and watched its new blossom kick awhile before turning its dead face to the sun.

Turning from the tree and limping badly, Jed approached the horse he had appropriated from the dead nester. He had already transferred the saddle bags, which meant he still had one warrant to serve. This fact made no sense to him, but he found himself considering it, nevertheless, as he dragged his right thigh painfully across the cantle, then straightened in the saddle. His wound had long since re-opened, and his entire right leg was now covered with a thick, heavy shield of blood.

He was hoping dimly that he might be able to pull his horse around and proceed alone back up over the ridge to the Lazy 8—to serve that warrant, of course. It was unlikely he would be able to manage such a trick, but he felt he should try, anyway. He was also dimly aware that he was not thinking too clearly.

And then—like a knife slashing away cobwebs—came Natalie's terrible, keening scream.

Jed glanced up the slope. On the ridge were two riders. One was Natalie, the other her father. Both of them, Jed suddenly realized, must have been alerted by the

202

distant rattle of gunfire earlier and had gone in search of Carl.

Natalie was outlined clearly against the sky. Jed saw her bury her face in her hands so she would not have to look on her brother's slowly twisting body. But Harlow rose in his saddle and cried out to Will Sukeforth:

'Sukeforth! I'm coming for you now!'

Brewster spurred his horse on down the long slope toward them, his big Colt gleaming in the sunlight as he brandished it. Jed was closer to Brewster, some distance higher on the slope than Will Sukeforth. He glanced down and saw Will thrust two revolvers into his belt and leap astride his horse. Someone handed up to him a Greener. Coolly Will broke it and checked the load. Then he urged his horse into a quick, hunching gallop up the slope toward the oncoming Harlow Brewster.

Jed found himself riding hard toward them. He had the dim notion that somehow he should prevent this, that there had already been enough—and more than enough— bloodshed. Perhaps it was the realization, too, that Natalie was above them on the ridge witnessing this confrontation with mounting horror. How much, after all, could the girl stand?

But he might as well have tried to stop a thunderbolt from striking the earth. Brewster was already firing at Sukeforth. Jed saw Sukeforth fold slightly as a round tore into his

203

right side. But Sukeforth kept coming. Another shot from Brewster plucked the nester's hat from his head. Lowering his head, Will brought up the Greener. Another round caught Will, this time high on his left shoulder. He bucked slightly, lowering the shotgun for a split second, but drove on still closer to the hard-riding Brewster.

Abruptly, Sukeforth fired the Greener, both barrels, its detonation—even in the open—awesome. Harlow Brewster flung up his arms. The buckshot caught him low and swept him backward off his horse. He appeared to land in two distinct impacts, as if an invisible scythe had sliced completely through him.

That should have been the end of it.

But down from the ridge swept Natalie, a Winchester across her pommel. Sukeforth, looking ragged, was about to turn his horse when he saw her coming. Riding with remarkable skill, Natalie aimed the Winchester and fired at Will. The shot went wild, and Jed saw her clutching frantically at her reins as the detonation from her rifle caused her horse to veer sharply to the right.

The horse bucked slightly and Natalie had to drop her Winchester in order to regain control of the skittish animal. Still on his horse, Will turned his mount completely about and started up the slope toward Natalie, pulling from his belt one of the big

Colts Jed had seen him place there a moment before. Natalie saw him coming and tried to pull her horse around to meet him.

From the moment he saw Natalie break from the ridge, Jed had been riding hard to intercept her. Now, as Will Sukeforth tried to get a bead on Natalie, his face frozen into a mask of hate, Jed called out to him, ordering him to drop the gun.

Jed was within five yards of Will by this time, and Jed's sharp command momentarily distracted him. That moment was all Jed needed. Sweeping alongside the man, Jed reached out and struck the Colt from Sukeforth's hand. Then he leaned over and grabbed the reins in an attempt to halt Sukeforth. He heard Natalie's scream and looked back to see Will had pulled out the second weapon. The big Colt thundered in his hand, and Jed felt the slug whisper past his cheek.

Jed flung himself off his horse at Stukeforth. He hit the nester solidly in the chest and drove him backward off his mount. Jed hit the ground a few feet from Will. Scrambling to his feet, Jed flung himself on Will, wrestled the Colt from his iron grip and flung it into the grass. Then he rolled Sukeforth over roughly—and found himself staring into the eyes of a dead man.

★　　　★　　　★

A shadow fell over Jed. Glancing up, he saw Natalie, eyes wild, her retrieved rifle in her hand, its muzzle aimed at his head. He looked into the rifle's bore and understood. Natalie had just seen her father killed and not too far from her at that moment her brother was twisting slowly in the sun. She was obviously no longer able to think clearly. Was not Jed part of those forces arrayed against her?

But she could not pull the trigger.

Gently, Jed reached out and took the Winchester from her. Then he straightened up, using the rifle as a makeshift crutch. It was then he caught sight of Tim Foley and the small posse he had rounded up sweeping onto the flat below them. He turned around. Zeke Summerworth and the rest of the nesters were off their horses, scrambling up the slope toward them.

'Zeke!' Jed called. 'Cut down Brewster! And bring the other bodies to the Lazy 8. The party's over!' As he spoke, he pointed down at the oncoming posse.

Zeke took one look, then hauled up and began issuing orders to those around him. Jed looked back at Natalie.

'I've reopened my wound, Natalie,' he told her softly. 'I need your help. Would you take me back with you to the Lazy 8?'

Natalie looked at him, as if she were seeing

him for the first time, then slowly nodded. Tears appeared in her eyes. She blinked. 'Yes, Jed,' she said swiftly.

He reached out and she fell sobbing into his arms. He had difficulty holding her and keeping himself upright on the Winchester at the same time, but he managed. He was pleased Natalie was going to cry a lot in the weeks and months to come, he knew. She was going to bend and almost snap. But she wasn't going to break.

And when the time came there was something he knew he was going to have to tell her.

CHAPTER TWELVE

It was two months later when Tim Foley ducked his head into Jed's office.

'I just saw Natalie Brewster ride in,' the deputy told him.

'Thanks,' Jed told him. 'Now make yourself scarce. I'll see you later at the Cattleman.'

Tim nodded and was gone.

Jed had sent Tim out to the Lazy 8 a week ago with a note asking Natalie to stop in and see him the next time she came to Sundown for supplies. This was the next time, and Jed was now bracing himself for what lay ahead.

207

For almost a week following her father's death, Natalie and her Indian housekeeper had nursed Jed in the big empty house. Natalie had tended to him in a kind of daze all that time. It was only as he was leaving that she began to come around to the stark reality of what had happened, not only to her father and her brother, but to the Lazy 8. Her grief and anger then had been painful to witness.

Jed had been glad to leave the place. He knew that Natalie now needed to be alone with her anguish.

But in recent weeks, Jed had seen her in town on various errands. She had dropped in to see him on each occasion, and he could tell she was over the worst of it. And so, reluctantly, he had sent Tim out with that note.

He fussed aimlessly at the papers and dodgers strewn over his desk, then paced a while in the small office, before sitting back down at his desk and telling himself to calm down. Natalie would need to know what Jed had to tell her—and there was no way he could avoid the necessity of telling her.

He was reaching into his lower drawer for the bottle of Maryland rye he kept there when Natalie stepped through the open door. He slammed the drawer shut and got quickly to his feet.

'Sit down, Natalie,' he told her. 'You got

my note?'

She smiled uncertainly. 'Yes, Jed. Is . . . is something wrong?'

'Sit down, Natalie.'

She hesitated a moment, then sat in the chair beside his desk. As always, her dark, lustrous beauty disturbed him. Her complexion had regained its creamy smoothness, her dark hair its sheen, her eyes their brilliance. And there was something else now—something almost indefinable. Maturity. Fullness. Undoubtedly it was the events of the past months. They had not broken her; they had turned her from a willful girl into a woman.

Jed sat down at his desk facing her. 'Natalie,' he began gently, 'I've waited to go over this with you because . . . I didn't want to open old wounds until I thought you were ready.'

She smiled wanly. 'You think I'm ready now.'

'I hope so.'

She straightened herself up in the chair and looked Jed squarely in the eyes. Her gaze was unwavering, almost defiant. 'Let's have it, Jed.'

'You think you killed Clayt Durant.'

Her eyes went cold. 'I did,' she snapped.

'No, Natalie,' he told her. 'You didn't.'

Her eyes widened. She leaned forward in her seat. 'But I told you! I shot him. I grabbed his gun and shot him with it.'

'Yes. You did that. And then you flung down the revolver and ran from the shack, mounted up, and rode like hell for the Lazy 8.'

'Yes,' she said, in a hushed voice. 'That's just how it was.'

Jed leaned back in his chair. 'Are you sure?'

'Of course, I am. Jed, why are you doing this?'

'Just answer my questions, Natalie.'

'All right.' Her face had grown pale, but her eyes did not waver as she regarded him.

'You say you ran from the line shack and went straight to your horse. But think. Are you sure you didn't get your Winchester from your saddle scabbard and return to the line shack, see that Clayt was still alive, and shoot him one more time in the back?'

A hand flew to her mouth. 'No, Jed,' she gasped. 'I did not. I was in a rage when I shot Clayt. Furious. But all I wanted was to get away from there.'

Jed leaned close. 'Now, listen to this carefully. Did you hear a shot from the line shack as you rode off?'

Her eyes widened and her hand dropped from her face. 'Yes,' she said, her voice hushed. 'How did you know that? I thought it was Clayt firing at me from the shack as I rode off.'

'It wasn't Clayt, Natalie. It was the one who fired what Doc Wynant is sure was the fatal bullet.'

'Jed, this is all very confusing—and painful. What are you driving at? I killed Clayt, I told you. I saw him fall.'

'I'm not denying that, Natalie. Or the fact that you put three rounds into him. What I *am* saying is that your shots were not fatal. Sukeforth could have saved Clayt, according to Doc Wynant, if those had been Clayt's only wounds. What killed him was the last shot he took from behind. That shot you heard was not Clayt firing at you. It was the murderer, finishing what you had begun.'

'My God, Jed. Who was it?'

'I've been giving that question considerable thought, Natalie.' He paused, unwilling to go on. He thought of the bottle of rye in his drawer and wondered if now would not be a good time to offer Natalie some.

'Go *on*, Jed,' she said. 'Tell me. Who do you think it was?'

'Carl.'

Natalie slumped back in her seat, almost as if Jed had struck her. 'But that afternoon Carl went to Sundown. I saw him go. That's why Pa sent Clayt and I to the North Fork Pass.'

'Carl could have changed direction when he saw you and Clayt riding off together. He probably followed you to the line shack, heard the shots, and when you ran out, saw

211

Clayt was still alive and finished him off.'

'But *why*, Jed?'

'Don't you know, Natalie? Surely you must have known how jealous he was of Clayt. It seemed to him—and to most people in these parts—that soon you and Clayt Durant would be married, and Clayt, not Carl, would be running the Lazy 8 alongside your father.'

'Yes,' Natalie admitted, slowly nodding her head. 'Carl *was* jealous. He made it clear how he felt that same afternoon. He and Pa had a terrible row before Carl rode off.'

'I'm sorry about all this, Natalie. But I couldn't let you go on thinking you were the one who murdered Clayt.'

'But I *am* partly responsible, Jed.'

'I think what you did—protect yourself—was considerably different from what Carl did. He murdered Clayt and then let you think it was all your doing. That was very cruel, Natalie.'

Natalie got to her feet. 'This has not been easy for you, Jed. Thank you. Carl was not a very nice person. I cannot understand why he did the things he did, but he was my brother and I loved him. Will you believe me when I say he was not always as you knew him? Something happened. I don't know what it was. But it changed him, made him what you saw. I prefer to think of Carl as he used to be—before he turned so hard.' She smiled. 'And that's the way I'll always remember

212

him.'

She turned then and walked from his office. Jed followed her out and watched her walk down the boardwalk toward Gus Hiram's general store. The Lazy 8 ranch wagon was pulled up in front of it, and aproned clerks were loading into it bales of barbed wire. Jed had heard that Natalie had taken charge of her holdings and had hired back some of her old hands, that she had accepted the fact that the North Basin could no longer be considered open range.

As Jed watched her tall, striking figure disappear into the store, he found himself thinking seriously of riding out some afternoon.

Photoset, printed and bound in Great Britain by REDWOOD PRESS LIMITED, Melksham, Wiltshire